DEVASTATION

BY STRENGTH AND GUILE - BOOK 3

PAUL TEAGUE

JON EVANS

IMAGINARY BROTHER

1

"Vengeance, we have a critical problem over here on *Orion*," said a voice from the stricken battleship.

The bridge of *Vengeance* was silent. After the near euphoria of their unexpected victory over the enemy battle fleet, the news from *Orion* was a harsh return to reality. The crew had given up hope of victory, but in the final moments of the battle, the tide had turned and the enemy had been vanquished. For now.

"Are you hearing us, *Vengeance*?" said the voice again. "We have a really serious problem over here."

Stansfield's attention snapped back into focus. He'd taken a minute away from the pressure of command. Sixty solitary seconds in which the constant bombardment of questions, problems and crises had faded away. But now it was time to take control once again.

"What's the issue, Captain Ryan?" asked Stansfield.

"That final explosion has critically damaged *Orion*'s nuclear containment system. I'm down here now, and there's a massive fracture in the housing."

"And the background noise?" Stansfield asked. Above the persistent pulse that seemed to permeate everything, there was an awful metallic groaning.

"Stress to the central framework, I think," said Ryan. "*Orion* has scores of hull breaches and is still venting atmosphere, and every time something fails it loads more stress on–"

"Spare me the technical details, Captain," said Stansfield. "I get the picture. Tell me there's some good news."

"Not much," admitted Ryan, "but twenty-three per cent of the survivors have either moved to *Vengeance* or are in transit. We've resumed shuttle transfers now the fighting is over, but we don't have the equipment or resources to calculate how long we have till the ship finally blows."

Stansfield ground his teeth. "What's the likely blast radius?"

Ryan paused. "The operating parameters for *Orion* are need-to-know only, sir. I can't release that information."

"Dammit, man," said Stansfield, anger getting the better of him, "just give me the damned numbers so I know what's at stake! Yours isn't the only ship affected by this."

There was another pause before Ryan finally replied. "If the main systems fail, the radiation release is likely to be fatal up to three hundred kilometres, sir."

"So you're telling me that if *Orion* blows, she'll kill everyone on *Vengeance* as well?"

"Affirmative," said Ryan.

"Damned if we move, damned if we stay," muttered Stansfield, shaking his head. The situation was impossible. If he stayed close to *Orion,* he risked losing *Vengeance*, but moving clear of the blast zone risked losing *Orion*'s survivors.

"They're all cloned, sir," said Commander Vernon, speaking so quietly that only Stansfield heard. "When push comes to shove, a cloned life is worth a little less, wouldn't you say?"

A cold view, but logical. Vernon might be right, but that didn't make the loss of life any more palatable, not to Stansfield. He shook his head.

"Doesn't matter. What if we end up fighting that armada with only a skeleton crew of pilots and Marines, Ed? And I'm mindful of *Vengeance*'s crew, the ones who've stayed with us through stasis and have only one life. I'd like to return them to Earth so they can enjoy their retirement."

Vernon nodded. He was no keener to sacrifice lives – even clones – than Stansfield, but his job was to raise the ugly, distasteful options. "Then we need to get Fernandez to *Orion* with a Tech Team," he said. "Find out how long we have before *Orion* goes critical."

"Agreed," said Stansfield. "Ryan, *Vengeance* is standing by. We'll send more people to help with the evacuation." He cut the channel before Ryan could respond, and opened another. "Lieutenant Fernandez, what's your status?"

"Engineering systems are clear of the malware, sir," said Fernandez. "My teams are working to restore operation to critical systems, and there's a lot to be done."

"Understood. I need you on *Orion*," said Stansfield.

"Sir?" said Fernandez, and the confusion was evident in his voice.

Stansfield outlined the situation and the proposed solution.

"That's a lot to ask, sir," said Fernandez. "The chances of achieving anything useful seem–"

"I don't want to hear it, Lieutenant," snapped Stansfield. "I know what I'm asking, but there's too much at stake, and you're the best man for the job."

"Thank you, sir," said Fernandez. "I understand."

"Then get moving," said Stansfield. "I want you on *Orion* and giving me updates in twenty minutes."

"Yes, sir," said Fernandez. "Are we cleared to use all ships now that we have control of the Battle Sphere? If the Mechs' ships have been destroyed, it should be safe to use any type of vessel."

"Agreed," said Stansfield. "Get every shuttle moving. I want *Orion* evacuated as soon as possible."

"Will do, Admiral."

"You did good work today, Lieutenant. The whole crew has made exceptional efforts."

Fernandez had a brief moment of smugness before Stansfield continued.

"But you're going to need ten times that resource or more when the Mechs' armada gets here, so let's get moving. The sooner we evacuate *Orion*, the sooner we're ready for that fleet."

"Understood, sir," said Fernandez.

"Keep me informed, Lieutenant." Stansfield closed the channel and looked around the bridge.

"We have activity at the portal, sir," said Lieutenant Yau, *Vengeance*'s Chief Science Officer. "It's beginning to open again."

"What is it with these Mechs?" said an exasperated Vernon. "It's open – close – open – close ... they can't make up their minds!" The commander was pissed. It had been one hell of a shift on the bridge, and he was overdue for a double espresso and a hot meal.

"I'm sure there's a logic to it, Commander," said Stansfield, no less anxious for the day to be over than his second in command. "I think they've been testing their systems, and they closed the portal to trap us here and block our reinforcements. If it's opening again, that probably means the Mechs' armada will be arriving soon."

"That's not the best news I've heard today," said Vernon with a grumpy frown.

"Quite," said Stansfield. He lowered his voice. "I don't have to tell you how dire this situation is," the admiral went on. "We need to fight dirty if we're to come out on top, and even then there's no guarantee."

Vernon nodded. "What did you have in mind?"

"I want you to lead the defence," said Stansfield. "Co-ordinate the teams on the Battle Sphere, make sure we have control, and get every fighting vessel, platform and mine out there."

"Against that armada, it might do no more than irritate them," Vernon pointed out.

"Then we need to irritate them so much they head for home," said Stansfield, an edge of iron in his voice. "They can't pass through the portal, Ed, they just can't. We have to stop them. Because if we don't, we know what happens next."

Vernon nodded. The Mechs would head for Sol, and with the Royal Navy entirely engaged in the war against the Deathless, there would be a massacre. It didn't bear thinking about.

"We do," said Vernon. "Whatever it takes." He and Stansfield shared a nod of understanding. "We'll need power, and if Fernandez is on *Orion*..."

"The situation is sub-optimal," agreed Stansfield, "but we do what we must, right?"

"Sir," said Vernon. "I'm on it." The commander stepped away to review his resources and begin the final defence.

Stansfield looked around his battered bridge. The crew had been through more than anyone could have asked of them, but the fight wasn't yet over.

"Listen up," said Stansfield, raising his voice so that it carried across the bridge. "We've been through a lot over the last few days, and it isn't going to get any better. There's nobody I'd rather have with me to make this stand, but our only hope is to work together like we've never worked before. The next few days will decide our fate and, if we fail, the fate of all we hold dear."

He paused to look around at the bridge crew. Telling it straight was one thing, but hope was vital.

"We're outnumbered, out-gunned, and stuck in a pair of crippled vessels further from home than any Royal Navy vessel has ever been. But we have a determination unmatched by our enemy, and the skill to come through this and win. With your help, that's exactly what I plan to do.

"Settle in, people, it's going to be a long day."

He gave them a nod, and they turned back to their stations. The atmosphere on the bridge lifted slightly.

"Sir," said Midshipman Pickering at the weapons console, who was monitoring *Vengeance*'s remaining long-distance sensors, "there's a change in the armada array."

Stansfield's head whipped round. Change was unwelcome. He turned to Lieutenant Yau. "Give me a visual on the enemy armada, Lieutenant."

"Ay, sir, on screen now," said Yau.

Yau moved his fingers over his console and the image of the wrecked *Orion*, still locked in the tight embrace of *Target Six*, was replaced with an enhanced long-range view of the approaching armada.

"What are we looking at?" asked Stansfield.

"The same ships as before," said Yau, "but in a different formation."

"I need details," said Stansfield. "What are we seeing?"

"I count at least six ship types," said Yau. "We've already encountered their battleships, and there are plenty of those in this fleet, but the purposes of the other ship types are unknown."

"Zoom in, please, Lieutenant," said Stansfield.

Yau zoomed in on a cluster of unidentified ship types.

"We don't know what's inside those battleships," said Vernon, momentarily distracted from his own plans. "I'd bet they carry a mix of Mechs with those disc things they use, and larger transports and weapons platforms. Fighters, maybe."

"Agreed, Commander," said Stansfield.

"I'll factor that into my planning," said Vernon before muttering, "although I've no idea how to respond."

"Ideas, please," said Stansfield, throwing the question open to his bridge crew.

"They look like they're moving house, sir," said Dyson from his console.

"You're from *Orion*?" said Stansfield. "Part of the relief crew?"

"Yes, sir," said Dyson. "Midshipman Terry Dyson, sir. I'm a systems support officer, with special knowledge of historical warfare."

"You're a historian?" said Stansfield, not bothering to hide his scepticism.

"Yes, sir, by academic qualification with a speciality in interstellar dispersal and exploration. This looks like a relocation to me, not a random armada."

"Elucidate, please, Midshipman," said Stansfield.

Dyson cleared his throat, suddenly aware that he had the attention of everyone on the bridge. "Well, er, conventionally, armadas are made up of fighting ships, but a fleet of this size" – he gestured at the screen, where the ship recognition system had classified a huge number of vessels – "can't be a battle formation."

"Why not?" said Vernon without looking up from his slate.

"Because they're too close together, sir," said Dyson. "Battleships operate individually and typically remain separated while travelling, only coming together at the point of action; travelling fleets remain close to each other, to be able to offer assistance and simplify inter-vessel transfers."

Vernon looked up, deeply sceptical, and shared a glance with Stansfield. They were both familiar with the theory of naval warfare, and it was a little disconcerting to be reminded of it by a mere midshipman.

"Civilians have a different agenda, sir," said Dyson. "Comfort, efficiency and convenience are more important than speed or stealth."

"So they're migrating?" said Vernon. "Like birds?"

Dyson looked uncertain, and glanced at Lieutenant Yau as if searching for help.

"Please," said Yau graciously, "you have the floor, Midshipman."

"Er, well, no, sir. Not like birds," said the suddenly reluctant Dyson. "Birds divide their time between two locations and migrate between them. These ships are too many, too varied."

"They look like Ark ships," said Lieutenant Yau. He flicked his hands at his console, zooming the images on the main display and super-imposing a measure. "These ships are huge, a kilometre across and five hundred metres deep. There's no way to know, but they could be three kilometres or more in length. They might hold hundreds of thousands of individuals. Millions, maybe. And there are dozens of these ships."

"Millions?" said Stansfield quietly, not quite able to wrap his head around the concept.

"But they can't all be combat troops," said Dyson, as if he were working through a tricky exam question. "The ships are too big. Civilians, probably, and all they possess." Dyson's face lit up as if he'd solved the problem. "Think back to your history classes, sir: the photographs of people with their possessions in a horse-drawn cart, or a car piled high with boxes on a roof rack. This is the alien equivalent. This is a population on the move."

There was an uncomfortable pause before the admiral spoke again. "So they're looking for somewhere to settle?" said Stansfield.

Yau shook his head, his face suddenly white. "No, they sent a battle fleet to secure the portal because they mean to pass through."

"They're not *looking* for a new home," said Vernon, "they already know where they're going. Earth."

Stansfield looked from Dyson to Yau to Vernon and back again. "Well, thank you, gentlemen," he said drily. "I've seldom had such an abrupt comedown after a victory."

There was an embarrassed silence on the bridge until the admiral spoke again. "Well? What are you waiting for? You have your orders," he snapped, "and we won't win by watching the clock run down."

2

―――――――

"As soon as we link up with the others," said Conway with feeling, "we stick together. Charlie Team fight as one unit."

They'd watched as explosions flared by *Orion*, monitoring the comms channels as the battle had played out beyond their reach. Like the rest of *Vengeance*'s crew, they had hoped for a few moments of calm in the stillness of space, but the Mechs weren't on board with that plan.

"Agreed," said Davies, the only other member of Charlie Team on the Battle Sphere. "Who knows what those lazy bastards are getting up to without us to guide them?" He eased himself around a column so that he could peer down the stairwell towards the secondary control rooms.

"You sure about this?" said Ten from the landing below. He and Gray were taking point as the team advanced downwards through the Battle Sphere, leaving Captain Figgis and his company on the floors above.

"No, I'm bloody not," snapped Davies. "I've no fucking idea if it'll work, or if we'll be able to stop the Mechs from taking back control, but it's the only bloody idea I've got."

It had come to him suddenly, like all the best ideas. The Battle

Sphere was an amalgam of the five original Firewall Spheres. Its command systems had been comprehensively trashed by the conflict between Davies and the Mechs as they both strove to take control. The damage was irreparable, and so the Sphere floated, its weapon systems offline and its engines powered down.

"But what if," Davies had said in a sudden burst of manic activity, "what if the four other control rooms are mechanically offline but in working order? Isolated, but operational."

"Just waiting to be remembered and plugged in?" Conway had asked, not even bothering to hide her scepticism. But Davies had seen a possible solution, so Charlie Team was heading downstairs to try to take control of an offline command room.

"Okay, okay," said Ten as he edged towards the door. "Just wanted to check." Gray slid into position on the other side of the door. "Three, two, one," said Ten, mashing the controls.

The doors slid open to reveal a control room almost identical to the one upstairs. But this one also had a squad of Mechs, who were carefully disassembling the larger pieces of equipment and loading the components onto trolleys.

"Contact," whispered Ten as he squeezed the trigger. The nearest Mech collapsed back in a spray of oil and blood, slumping over a trolley. Ten fired again and again as he worked his way into the room. Gray was firing as well, working her side of the room and targeting the Mechs that were hauling cables and boxes through a hole in the wall.

The Mechs fell back, scrambling for weapons but falling quickly. In seconds it was all over, and silence fell. Ten moved across the room, checking the corpses, while Gray positioned herself at the doors on the far side, away from the stairs.

"That went well," said Ten as Conway and the others came in from the stair well. "And they've done half the work for us," he said, gesturing at the trolleys.

Davies snorted as he hurried across the room, rifle slung. He hauled a Mech corpse off a trolley and shoved it into a corner, then crouched down to inspect the equipment. "Looks like they're salvaging the same parts we are," he said. "That's the comms-link box, I think, and those things over there are guidance and targeting computers."

"Knew this wouldn't work," said Jackson from his station near the stairs. "The Mechs plan to lock us out just as we plan to lock them out."

"Shit," said Gray.

"Doesn't matter," said Conway. "In fact, it validates Double-D's idea. We keep going and make our stand upstairs as planned, right?"

"I've got nothing better," said Davies. Ten nodded his agreement.

"Motion carried," said Conway. "Davies, get the equipment upstairs. I'll update the admiral and check in on *Vengeance*."

"On it," said Davies, already sorting through the stacked kit before pushing one of trolleys towards the stairs.

Conway watched for a few seconds, then turned away and opened a channel to the bridge of *Vengeance*.

"Conway," said Lieutenant Yau, "good to know you're still alive. What can we do for you?"

Conway outlined the plan in concise sentences as Davies and Jackson started lugging equipment upstairs.

"Solid plan," said Yau when Conway had finished. "I've nothing to add, and it fits with what's going on over here." He gave her a quick summary of *Orion*'s situation.

"Understood, sir," said Conway.

"Is there anything else you need from us at the moment?"

"No, sir," said Conway. "We'll lock down the Battle Sphere, then evac in the shuttles. No idea how long we'll be."

"Make it quick, Conway," said Yau. "We've no idea how long we have till *Orion* fails."

"Roger, Conway out." She closed the channel. "I need to update Captain Figgis," she said. "You okay here?"

"Oh, we're just dandy," said Ten. "Don't worry about us."

"Yeah, wasn't actually worried," said Conway, "just being polite." She turned to leave, grabbing an unidentifiable piece of equipment as she moved towards the door.

"What about the other control rooms?" said Ten suddenly, pointing at the floor. There were three more control rooms, one for each of the five original Battle Spheres. "They'll all have the same kit, won't they?"

Conway swore and turned back.

"The Mechs'll just raid them now that we've taken this one, won't they?" said Ten. "We'll be back to square one."

"Yeah, we'll need to close them all down," said Conway. "I'll send Jackson down to help and see if Figgis will spare a couple of squads." She looked at Ten from behind her faceplate and gestured at the rest of the room. "Can I leave the rest of this to you?"

"No worries," said Ten happily. "Fire and brimstone, all the way down, and no toys for the Mechs to play with."

"Unless they've got more stores," said Jackson as he collected another piece of kit from the trolley, "or automated fabrication units, or redundant backups."

Ten and Conway watched him leave. "He's a joyous ray of sunshine, that one," said Ten.

But Conway was already on her way. "Burn it down, Ten," she said on the way out, "all of it."

"My favourite phrase," said Ten.

3

"*Vengeance*, this is *Orion*." Ryan's voice was tight with stress and worry.

"Go ahead, *Orion*," said Lieutenant Yau.

"I don't know how to say this," said Ryan, "but we seem to be under threat from boarders." He sounded almost personally aggrieved by the admission.

"Elaborate, please, Captain," said Admiral Stansfield.

"Mechs from *Target Six*," said Ryan. "Hundreds of them. We think they're on the outside of the hull, looking for a way in."

"Are you sure?" asked Stansfield, frowning across the bridge at Vernon. Another boarding operation was a nuisance they could ill afford. "Our analysis showed that *Target Six* was incapacitated."

"Well, there's something going on," said Ryan. "She's floating only a few hundred metres away, and there are Mechs spewing from her like rats from a sinking ship."

"Ha, good one, sir," said Yau.

"What?" snapped Ryan, clearly in no mood for a joke.

Stansfield glared at Yau and shook his head. "Where's Lieutenant Fernandez? Has he left yet?"

"No, sir," said Yau, serious and straight-faced again. "Pre-flight checks are in progress, he should be away in a few minutes."

"Fine." Stansfield turned to Commander Vernon. "Get Hunter and the rest of Charlie Team on that shuttle, and send over whatever Marines we can spare."

Vernon frowned down at his slate and sniffed. "The squads that were working with Charlie Team to clear the OctoBots are available," he said, "those that are still alive."

"Send them," said Stansfield. "Captain, we're sending you some help."

"Help?" said Ryan. "What help?"

Stansfield grinned evilly. "A penal Marine and his team. I think you're going to get on marvellously."

F light Lieutenant Haworth watched the portal opening with a sense of foreboding. From his station in one of *Vengeance*'s larger bays, he could watch the preparations as shuttles and the remaining fighting craft were prepped for combat.

But there was something different about the portal this time. Many years piloting everything from a Raptor to a fast attack craft had taught him that, in space, different was never a good thing.

There was a ping as a new channel was opened.

"Haworth," said the voice of Commander Vernon. "Prep for immediate launch. Flight plan to follow."

"Roger that, sir," said Haworth. "What are the Mechs playing at now? And do we have any idea where the portal gets its power from?"

But Vernon had already closed the channel, and Haworth took the absence of an answer as a negative. The portal had opened to about a quarter of its usual diameter, but it looked different this time around. Bright green flashes ran across its mouth like dancing sparks.

Haworth hurried his team from the ready room, where they'd been studying feeds from the few remaining external sensors on

Vengeance's hull. "Move it, people," he said, ushering them to their small fleet of ships. "It's time to work for a living."

"Again?" asked some wag in the small crowd. Haworth ignored them.

"Haworth, hold on," came a shout as the flight team were making final checks of their suits and kit. Fernandez was jogging across the bay, already wearing a powered engineering suit. Behind him was a squad of armoured Marines, all with large kit bags.

"I've got a bad feeling about this," said Lieutenant George as the Marines clattered to a halt.

"We need a lift," said Fernandez, "to *Orion*."

Haworth stared for a moment. Then a message with the subject line *New Orders* pinged into his HUD.

"Just a moment," he said, raising a finger. He scanned the message and grunted. "Right. You know we're a fighting squadron, not transport?"

"What do we look like?" said a Marine in battle-scarred armour. "The comic relief?"

Haworth stared at the Marines for a few long seconds. "You sure about this? Word is that *Orion's* not got long to live."

"Hours, probably," said Fernandez. "But if these guys don't get there soon, the Mechs might have slaughtered the rest of the crew before they can be evacuated, so...?"

"Fine," said Haworth with a resigned nod. "Shuttle *Holborn* leaves in two minutes," he said, pointing across the bay at one of the newer shuttlecraft. "But she's coming straight back with rescued crew. Might be a while before we're able to bring you back, and that's if we don't get wiped out ourselves."

"Good enough for me," said Fernandez, and he led the Marines across the bay to *Holborn*.

~

Holborn turned out to be more of a freight carrier than a personnel shuttle, but with only the Marines aboard, she managed a fair turn of speed.

"Not exactly comfortable," said Hunter as *Holborn* manoeuvred around the bulk of *Vengeance*'s hull. The Marines were all in the shuttle's cargo bay, holding on to the fixtures and straps that were usually used to secure the goods that *Holborn* carried.

"Manoeuvring almost complete," said the pilot, Lieutenant Carter, over the shuttle's public channel. "Sixty-second main engine burn coming up, followed by a few seconds of manoeuvring, then a seventy-second engine burn to put us alongside *Orion*."

"Alongside?" said Fernandez in alarm. "Don't you mean 'inside' and safely docked?"

"Didn't Haworth tell you?" said Carter as the Marines shuffled and grumbled in the cargo bay. "We're going in fast to pick up suited crew members near the front of the ship. We aren't going to the main bay."

"Great," said Mason. "There's nothing I like more than a little spacewalk."

"In a warzone," added Hunter.

"Yeah, in a fucking warzone."

"Firing now," said Carter, ignoring the complaints.

The engines roared and the shuttle kicked forward, throwing the Marines against their restraints and raising another round of complaints and swearing.

"Manoeuvring for final burn," said Carter a minute later. "Hold on to your horses."

The main engines cut off, and the force on the Marines fell away. Then the manoeuvring thrusters fired and the shuttle spun on its axis, battering the Marines against the top of the cargo bay.

"Bloody hell!" said Hunter as he was thrown against the ceiling. "We need to get there in one fucking piece!"

But if Carter heard, he gave no sign of listening. "Second burn firing now." The shuttle stopped spinning as suddenly as it had started, but before the Marines could recover, the main engines had fired again, slamming them back against their restraints.

"I'm not flying with this airline again," moaned Mason. "Even my bruises have bruises."

"Quit whining," said Kearney as she fought to hold on to her kit bag. "And get ready to go as soon as the doors open."

"Ten seconds," said Haworth as the interminable engine burn continued. "Five, four, three, two, one." The force pressing the Marines against their restraints disappeared, and they floated free.

"Slight correction," said Haworth as the doors on the side of the shuttle opened to show a view of stars and distant nebulae.

"Always get me," said Kearney as she stared into the vacuum, with only the thin faceplate of her helmet between her and a grisly death.

Then the shuttle spun gently and *Orion*'s hull appeared, battered and scarred, only twenty metres away.

"Tethers away," said Haworth as two lines shot silently across the void to attach themselves to *Orion*. A hatch opened beside the lines' anchor points, and a suited figure waved at *Holborn*.

Kearney waved back, then pushed herself through the doorway, her bag floating behind her on a short cable. She grabbed the tether and pulled herself across the open space, swinging inelegantly into the airlock on the other side.

"Made it," she breathed as friendly hands caught her and guided her into the ship. The airlock was crowded – thirty people, at least – and the arrival of the Marines with their bulky armour and kit wasn't making life any easier.

"You're from *Vengeance*?" said a voice. Kearney looked around for the speaker, searching amongst the suits in the airlock until her HUD identified the person who'd sent her the message and pinned a label in her view: Midshipman York, Engineering.

"We are," said Kearney as the crew began to haul themselves across the void, moving quickly. "Anything you need?"

York gave a thin laugh, and Kearney heard the fear in the midshipman's voice. "A working ship," she said, "but I guess that's too much to ask right now."

"Sorry," said Kearney. "You'll be safe on *Vengeance*."

"Really?" said York. "Somehow, I doubt it. Why are you here?"

Kearney gave her a quick rundown of the mission as the last of the Marines arrived. "Time for you to go," she said, nodding at the open hatchway.

But York hesitated. Then she waved her hand. "No, I'm staying," she said. "You'll need me to get through the ship."

"We have the plans, York," said Fernandez impatiently. "Go now. That's an order."

"The plans aren't the ship, sir," said York. "And with the damage, there are new problems." She pulled herself back towards the inner airlock. "I'll leave when you do, sir."

Fernandez was quiet for a moment, sizing her up. She was one of the few people in the group wearing something more substantial than the emergency environmental survival suits. Her engineering suit was designed for working in zero-G and vacuum, so she was at least as well-equipped as the rest of the team.

"Fine," said Fernandez, "you can start by cycling the airlock."

"Sir," said York. The outer hatch closed, and atmosphere hissed into the chamber. Then the inner hatch opened and the Marines floated out, past crew members still waiting to escape the stricken battleship. York led the team along a corridor as the last of the suited crew disappeared into the airlock.

"This is where we split up, sir," said Kearney to Fernandez as they reached a cross-corridor. "We go forward and up, you go that way," she said, pointing along the corridor.

"Except me," said Hunter. "Stansfield wants me to find Ryan and offer assistance. Let's go, team." And Hunter disappeared down a corridor with his small team, leaving the others at the junction.

"Why go that way?" said a confused York as Hunter vanished from sight. "There's nothing left that way."

"Mechs," said Kearney simply. "We're hunting Mechs."

Orion groaned, a horrible noise that sent tremors through the walls.

"And we don't have much time," said Fernandez. "Good luck, Trooper," he said to Kearney.

"You too, sir," she replied. "Let us know when you're done, and we'll see you in the main bay." She turned away as York led Fernandez and his team – two technicians from *Vengeance* and two Marines as bodyguards – along the corridor. In moments, they had disappeared from view.

"Thirty seconds," said Kearney to her team, "then we move out. Take the kit you can shift, leave the rest here."

The team bustled, checking weapons and ammunition and transferring equipment from kit bag to backpack.

"Time to go," announced Kearney, pulling up the route that would put them between the attacking Mechs and the retreating crew. "You want the van or the rear?" she said to Mason as she checked her rifle.

"Oh, I'll take the rear-guard," he said. "I've had plenty of fun today already."

Kearney nodded. "Right," she said, "no point hanging around." She kicked off from the wall and began making her way towards the Mechs.

"Here we go again," muttered Mason as he followed.

4

"Oh, I do like to be beside the seaside," sang Ten as he laced the equipment with explosives.

"Do you have to sing?" said Gray as she watched the corridor from the doorway. The Mechs hadn't been back, but it was only a matter of time. "It was bad enough when they were shooting at us, but the music really isn't helping."

"Sorry," said Ten, making the last adjustments to the detonators and syncing them to his HUD. "It helps distract me, sometimes. Right, done," he said, picking up his rifle. "On to the next one?"

"Don't we need to blow this room before we move on?" said Gray.

"Not, I think, while we're standing in it," said Ten. He moved towards the stairwell at the opposite end of the room from Gray. He eased open the door and peered out. Nothing.

"Shit, movement," said Gray, ducking into the control room and backing away from the doorway. She fired at something Ten couldn't see, and took another few steps.

"Move, Gray," said Ten. "I've got this."

She fired another burst, then turned and ran across the room, taking care to keep out of Ten's line of fire. As she ran, Ten fired past her, two short bursts.

Then she was past him and onto the landing. Jackson was there, crouching on the stairs above to fire through the open door at the Mechs that were flooding into the room.

"Time to go," said Ten, backing out and slapping an armoured fist onto the door controls. "Down we go," he said as the doors slid closed. He gestured at Jackson to move, and the three Marines darted down the stairs as Ten triggered the detonators.

There was a series of loud bangs from the control room as the explosives blew. Then there was an urgent hissing.

"Fire suppression system," said Jackson. "Hadn't expected that."

"Good to know the Mechs take fire safety seriously," said Ten, crouching at the bottom of the stairs outside the third control room. He paused long enough to update Conway and to allow Gray and Jackson to catch up; then he triggered the doors and barrelled into the control room.

"More contact," he said, triggering the underslung grenade launcher on his rifle. Behind him, Gray and Jackson were both firing, but clearly the Mechs had planned for this and now they returned fire, spraying the end of the control room and the stairs beyond.

Ten hit the floor, sliding behind a stack of equipment. Gray and Jackson dived the other way, and Ten sat facing the stairwell with his back to the equipment as the air filled with gunfire.

"This isn't good," shouted Jackson.

The Mechs fired indiscriminately, shredding the room in their eagerness to kill the Marines. Rounds tore at the equipment, ripping through the delicate components and filling the room with shrapnel.

"Grenades," yelled Ten, palming a device. He waited a few seconds, then threw a grenade towards the Mechs. He saw Jackson float across the doorway, firing as he went. Then the grenade exploded behind him and Ten heaved himself to his feet and charged back out of the room, ducking as he ran. He threw himself onto the landing as Gray triggered the door controls.

"That was too fucking close," said Ten as the doors slid shut. He punched out the empty magazine from his rifle and slotted in a new one.

"You reckon we can count that room as destroyed?" said Gray.

"Yeah, I reckon," said Ten.

"They'll be ransacking the rooms downstairs," said Jackson. "This was a trap, but they'll be waiting for us below as well."

"Nope," said Ten, looking out into the stairwell, "they're coming for us in numbers. Back, back!"

They scurried up the stairs, dropping grenades as they went to cover their retreat.

"How's it going, Davies?" said Ten as he reloaded his rifle again. "You done yet?"

"No," said Davies. "You?"

"Minor problems, if I'm honest." Ten squeezed off a burst of fire at a Mech that poked its head into view. "Control rooms two and three are toast, but there's a bit of a problem getting to the last two."

"This'll all have been for nothing if the Mechs work around us," said Conway, "so what are our options?"

A brace of Mechs ran up the stairs, firing as they came. They collapsed before reaching the top of the flight as Gray and Jackson fired down at them.

"They're still coming," said Jackson. "Can't see us getting out of this."

Gray tossed a couple of grenades down the stairs, watching till they bounced and tumbled out of sight. Two bangs sounded from below in quick succession. "Down again?" she asked. "Anyone free up there to help?"

"It's just the four of us," said Conway as she came down the steps. "Davies doesn't need me, and Figgis has the rest of this floor under control. There's a squad up there in case the Mechs get past us." She hefted her rifle. "On three?"

Davies hummed as he worked, replacing the damaged components in the control room with the good ones stolen from the room below. He moved quickly, focused on his task, but part of him couldn't help but think that he'd missed something important.

As the list of things to do grew steadily shorter, he had a sudden chill down his spine. His hand froze above a power converter, and for ten whole seconds he just stared at nothing.

"Oh, shit," he said finally. He *had* missed something important, but at least now he knew what it was. He flicked open a channel to the rest of the team. "Conway, we have a problem," he said.

"Bit busy here, Double-D," she said in response. "Bit of a firefight – shit, over there, left, left! And stay down, you bastard! – What did you – kill that fucker! – want, Davies?"

"The Mechs must have a control room of their own," said Davies.

"Tell us something we don't know," said Jackson.

"Right, but I'd assumed it was somewhere else, somewhere we hadn't been or seen," said Davies. "But it must be one of the five, and it must be as banged up as our own control room. That's why the Mechs were stripping room two – they needed the parts to repair room five."

"And what do – look out! – you want us to do with that information?" snapped Conway.

"Trash the last two control rooms, and they'll have to find another solution," said Davies. "We'll have won, they won't be able to take control of the Battle Sphere."

"What the fuck do you think we're trying to do down here, eh?" snapped Conway. "Just get things ready up there and let us focus on the shit down here. Conway out."

On the stairs outside control room four, Conway and the team were making little to no progress. The Mechs were there in huge numbers, and they showed no sign of leaving.

"This is a stalemate," shouted Conway over the roar as Gray and Jackson sprayed fire through the gap in the door from their position on the stairs. "We need to move forward!"

"Worse," said Ten, "because the Mechs win by default if we stay out here."

"Great, so what do we do?" said Conway.

Ten paused to launch a grenade into the control room; then he shook his head. "We aren't getting in this way, they're too well prepared. Get back, up the stairs," he said, taking a step. "I've got an idea."

The team retreated back to the landing outside control room three and regrouped. Gray reloaded her rifle as Ten searched through his pack and pulled out another pack of explosives and a bag of detonators. He set them out on the landing and hummed as he arranged them.

"What's the plan, Ten?" said Conway. The Mechs were still probing the stairs, but they seemed content to leave the Marines alone, both sides staying on their respective floors.

"Shaped charges," said Ten cryptically, not looking up from his work. He was rolling the plastic explosive into metre-long snakes, each with a detonator. "Help me with this, would you?"

Conway stared for a moment; then she slung her rifle over her shoulder and grabbed a block of explosive. "Brings back happy memories," she murmured as she worked, "but I still don't get the plan."

"Almost done," said Ten. He looked up. "We need to get that door open, and then we're going to lay a surprise for our mechanical friends."

"You two good with the stairs?" asked Conway.

"For now," said Jackson, "but it's only a matter of time before they overwhelm us. They're just girding their loins."

"As long as they do it down there," said Conway. "You ready?" she said to Ten.

He stood up and checked his rifles. "Good to go."

They moved to stand either side of the sliding doors into control room three as Gray launched another brace of grenades into the stairwell.

"On three," said Conway. "Three, two, one."

Ten punched the door control. Nothing happened. He punched it again, then a third time, just to be sure. "Nope, it's buggered," he said, offering his professional opinion. "I guess we did more damage than we thought."

"Figures," said Conway, slinging her rifle. She pulled out her knife and worked the blade between the doors, twisting it to open a gap she could force her armoured fingers into. She paused to glance at Ten; then she heaved on the door.

It slid open sixty centimetres, then stopped, jammed fast on something. Ten stuck his rifle into the gap and peered into the room. It was a mess of burned and broken equipment and cabinets, but nothing moved. He grabbed the second door and hauled it back, opening a gap that they could slide through into the ruined room.

"Wow," said Conway as she surveyed the damage. "You didn't hold back." Every cabinet had been punctured and ripped apart, their contents destroyed by the blasts and spread across the room.

"No point doing half a job," said Ten. He carried the explosive snakes into the room and began forming them against the floor, moving quickly to outline a large circle. Conway helped, kneading the plastic into shape and checking that the detonators were in position.

"Good, that'll do nicely," said Ten a few moments later as he stood back to admire their handiwork. "Blow out the floor, drop grenades into the room below, then down we go to finish the job."

"Down?" said Conway sceptically. "Is that really necessary?"

"Down," said Ten, "then down again, into room five. Destroy the lot, and the Mechs are screwed. Davies takes control, and we're home and dry."

Conway wasn't at all sure about that, but she kept her thoughts to herself. "Have we got enough explosives to go through the second floor?"

Ten gestured at the small pile of unused snakes. "Probably," he said, "but one problem at a time, right?"

Conway nodded, and they both backed out onto the landing. Ten carefully loaded the explosives into his pack, then switched back to his rifle.

"Fire in the hole," he said. Then he triggered the detonators. There was a series of loud bangs from the control room, then a drawn-out crash as a huge section of the floor collapsed into the room below.

"Grenades," said Ten, hurling several through the hole so that they bounced randomly around the room below. Conway followed suit, and they counted the explosions as the grenades went off.

"And in we go," said Ten as the last one exploded. He charged through the doorway and leapt into the hole, rifle in his hands. Conway was right behind him, and they stood back to back in the middle of control room four, firing at any Mechs not blasted apart or crushed beneath the falling floor.

The damage was extensive. Grenade shrapnel had shredded most of the remaining equipment and the Mechs who had been removing it. There was smoke everywhere, and the lights were out. In the darkened room, nothing was visible with the naked eye, and the Marines relied on their HUDs to see what was going on.

The door out into the Battle Sphere was half closed. Only shadows moved in the corridor beyond, but Ten fired at them anyway, chasing the Mechs away.

"They won't go far," said Ten. Then he spun around as the door at the other end of the room opened. Gray and Jackson stormed in, clearly expecting to find more organised opposition.

"That seemed to work," said Ten, slinging his rifle. He moved to a clear section of floor near the far door and set to work with the explosives, laying them as fast as he could. "A hand?" he said to Conway, who was watching. She shook her head and knelt by his side, laying out the explosives.

"That'll do," said Ten when all the explosives were wired up to their detonators.

"Will it?" said Conway. "Surely that's not going to take the floor out? And isn't it in the wrong place?"

But Ten was already hurrying towards the stairs as Gray and

Jackson fired through the smoke to cover the retreat. He turned at the door to the stairwell and gestured at Conway. "Are you coming?"

Confused, she followed Ten and joined the others on the landing. The doors slid shut behind her.

"We're going down the stairs," said Ten, reloading his rifle. "Fast as we can, no quarter given. Got it?"

The others nodded, happier now that they understood the plan.

"Here we go," said Ten, triggering the detonators. As soon as the first one fired, he charged down the stairs. Two surprised Mechs went down quickly, clearing the landing and the way to the fifth control room. As soon as they were all on the landing, Ten hit the controls and they surged into the room.

A bunch of Mechs were standing around, all firing their weapons into the small hole in the ceiling at the far end of the room, where the explosives had punched through. So intent were they on preventing another attack that they didn't notice the Marines until it was too late. Firing as they went, the team moved into the room and up the sides, shattering the Mechs and blasting them apart.

"And that's it," said Ten as the last Mech collapsed. He reloaded his rifle as he looked around, checking for threats. But the Mechs were all dead, and the equipment showed the same level of dismemberment and destruction as the kit in the first control room, where Davies still wrestled to regain control of the sphere.

"Our work here is done," Ten announced, well pleased with their efforts. He slung his rifle and yanked a Mech weapon from its owner's arms, turning it around until he worked out how to use it. Then he pointed the business end at the surviving equipment and emptied the magazine, playing it across equipment, cables and cabinets until there was nothing left but smoking ruins.

"Control room five is done, Davies," said Conway, "we're on our way back."

"That's good," said Davies, "because we've got a big fucking problem up here."

5

"No, looks like this way is blocked as well," said Midshipman York. She was staring through the glass of a pressure door, looking into the void behind as she attempted to guide Lieutenant Fernandez and the team to the reactors that powered the ship.

"Is there any damn job on this mission that's straightforward?" muttered Fernandez. "What is it this time?" he asked. "More fallen super-structure?"

So far, their attempts had been impeded mostly by twisted super-structure that either blocked corridors or warped the doors so that they wouldn't open. Deep in the ship, they should have had a clear path to the reactors, but the damage to *Orion* was so great that even short distances were problematic.

"Not so much fallen as, well, absent," said York, pushing away from the door and calling up the ship's plans. "I don't fancy going out there," she said as she marked up the damage on the plans and looked for another route.

Fernandez squeezed forward to see for himself. "Ah, yes. Let's find another route." On the far side of the door, there was a ten-metre gulf where something had torn a great hole in the hull. "This isn't a gap we should try to cross."

Their last detour had forced them towards the hull to work around a section of blast damage in the main crew quarters. Out here, near the edge of the ship, there were hull breaches and occasional gaping holes where the hull plating had been ripped completely away.

From far across the ship, they felt an explosion, and the entire structure shook and groaned.

"That's been happening on and off since the attack," said York. "I'd be worried about it, but it's small and a long way off."

Fernandez nodded, impressed by her detachment.

"This way," said York. They backtracked along the corridor and tried again, following a new route now that the AI in York's HUD knew about the damage. "Pity we can't get a proper damage report from the monitors," she added as she took them down another corridor and through a hallway, "but that would require a minimally operative ship."

Fernandez grunted his agreement. They'd spent a frustrating forty minutes trying to reach the reactor, a journey that should have taken only five, and they were still a hundred metres away.

"How much longer do we have, do you think?" asked Tofler, one of the technicians who'd volunteered for the mission. He and Hurley, the other technician, were towing bags of equipment that Fernandez hoped would be useful if they ever reached the reactor.

"Before she blows? Impossible to say," said Fernandez, idly checking his radiation meter. It showed nothing untoward, but that only really meant they weren't yet dead. There was plenty of time for that to change.

"Only Charlie Team are heavily engaged, and I'm guessing we're running short of options," said Tofler.

"What?" said Fernandez, snapped out of his thoughts by Tofler's comments. "How do you know?"

"Kearney's providing updates in a public channel," said Hurley. "Aren't you in that one?"

"No," said a frustrated Fernandez, "I am not." He flicked into his

HUD's menus, searching for the channel. Then an invitation arrived from Tofler, saving him the trouble. "Thanks," he muttered.

He flicked into the channel and scrolled through the updates. Kearney wasn't flooding the team with information, but she was posting news every few minutes, and it sounded like they'd found plenty of Mechs.

"So if we're going to do anything useful," said Tofler, "we probably need to do it sooner rather than later, sir."

"This looks good," said York as she led them through another intersection and into a long straight corridor. "There's a turn halfway down here; then we cut through the water tanks and we'll be almost there."

York opened two more doors, then floated out into a triple-height room. "This is it," she said, one hand on a surface, "water tank number four. You've got cutting equipment?" she said to Tofler.

"Hold on a moment," said Fernandez. "I thought you meant we would move between the tanks. You can't seriously mean to *swim* to the reactor?"

"It's this," said York, "or another long detour, or we risk a spacewalk."

Fernandez opened his mouth to speak, but wasn't sure he had any better ideas. He gave up. "Is it liquid?"

"Temperature is a solid three degrees in this room, so it should be, but would it make any difference?" said York.

"Probably not," conceded Fernandez. He waved Tofler forward. The technician had produced a small cutting torch from his kit bag, and he now clamped himself to the water tank.

"Here we go," he said, firing up the torch. It flared brighter than the sun as he touched it to the metal of the tank, but it cut through quickly, and in only a few moments they were peering through a metre-wide hole into a mass of black water.

"Dark," said York, apparently not so keen on this route any more.

It was weird seeing the water hang there, but without gravity to pull it around, there was nothing to force it from the tank. "If the AG comes back on now, we're screwed," said Hurley.

"How far?" asked Fernandez, playing his helmet lamps into the water.

"No more than five metres, straight across," said York. "You want to go first, sir?"

"Oh, sure," said Fernandez reluctantly, taking the torch from Tofler and checking the controls. "I guess this thing'll work underwater?"

"No problem with that, sir," said Tofler, "but it'll boil the water, and that could get a bit unpleasant."

"No hanging around, then," muttered Fernandez. "I'll signal when I'm clear." He took a deep breath, realised how ridiculous that was, then forced himself to breathe normally as he pushed into the tank. He kicked forward, thrashing against the water as he groped for the far wall.

It arrived more quickly than he had expected, and he banged into it despite his lights. Estimating distance in the weird, wet darkness wasn't easy.

"Made it, cutting now." Fernandez closed his eyes and flicked on the torch. Immediately, the water around the torch began to bubble and boil. Steam rushed away, making it difficult to hold the torch on the tank. Fernandez struggled to mimic Tofler's practised ease as the torch juddered and jumped around.

"Almost done," said Fernandez, hoping that this was true. If he'd cut in the wrong place, there was no way of knowing what damage he might have done to anything on the other side of the tank.

The torch wobbled around under the light from the suit's lamps until, finally, Fernandez completed the cut. He pushed at the tank wall and it moved, falling into the compartment beyond. He pulled at the edge of the hole, until his head emerged from the water and he could see the room on the other side of the tank. The emergency lights were still on, throwing a dim light across the huge room.

"Looks good," he said as he peered around, "but there's a vacuum here." He stowed the torch and heaved himself out into the room. Tofler and Hurley quickly followed, then York. Hurley had to play the torch into the water to stop it from freezing as the two Marines, Muller and Douglas, made it through the tank.

"Like being back on Dartmoor," said Muller as he banged his limbs to shake loose the ice that had formed on his armour as soon as he'd emerged into the reactor room.

"Warmer than Dartmoor," said Douglas, "but I'll bet there isn't a cream tea to be had anywhere close by."

"Knock it off," snapped Fernandez, who wasn't in the mood for the Marines' banter. "York, are we in the right place?"

"Yes," she said. "This is reactor two, one of a pair of Rietveld-Muers fast-form reactors that form *Orion*'s secondary power source."

The reactor room was huge, easily thirty metres across and twenty high. The reactor itself sat on a web of struts, hanging in mid-air like a great black stone. It was wrapped in foamcrete insulation and studded with sensors and pipes of various sizes and types.

"Ugly beast," muttered Tofler.

Fernandez couldn't help but agree. His radiation meter still showed nothing unusual, but he didn't want to hang around here for long. "Check the monitors," he said to Hurley, gesturing at a bank of machines that hugged the far wall. The reactors' control and monitoring systems were multiply redundant and battery-backed, so that there could never be a situation where it wasn't possible to inspect their behaviour.

"Yeah, this is definitely the faulty reactor," said Hurley. "Looks like everything's off the scale bad. Linking it through to the HUD comms."

A moment later, a new team channel appeared with information from the reactor's monitors.

"Shit," said Fernandez as he reviewed the information. "Why didn't we know all this before?" he asked angrily. The whole point of redundant monitors was to avoid situations like this.

"Not sure, sir," said Hurley, tapping away at a keyboard. "Hold on, yes, that's it. Looks like a general comms failure after the initial alerts were raised."

Fernandez frowned inside his helmet. "That shouldn't be possible."

Hurley shrugged. "You want me to work on it?"

"No," said Fernandez. "Do a full visual inspection of the reactor casing, support struts, couplings, everything. Find out what's gone wrong."

"Roger," said Hurley, pushing away from the keyboard and floating towards the reactor with Tofler.

Fernandez opened a channel back to *Vengeance*. "This is Fernandez. We're at the reactor and assessing the damage. That's all for now. Fernandez out."

"I don't like the look of that," said York, playing her lamps across a crack in the reactor's casing. "If that fails, the reactor goes bang and takes the ship with it."

There was a shudder as something exploded far away in the *Orion*'s guts. Above them, the reactor creaked, shifting its position as the vast struts that held it in place were twisted by *Orion*'s slow-motion collapse.

"She can't hold much longer, surely?" said Tofler from the far side of the reactor. "If I were Stansfield, I'd be getting *Vengeance* as far away as possible."

"I'm not sure you'd be saying that if you were one of the poor buggers still trapped on *Orion*," Fernandez reminded him.

"I *am* one of the poor buggers still trapped on *Orion*," pointed out Tofler. "Believe me, I don't want to be left behind, but the admiral isn't going to wait forever, is he?"

"Quite," said Fernandez. "Let's move things along, take our measurements and get some estimates for the admiral. Then we can head home, safe in the knowledge that we have plenty of time to clear the blast area."

"I thought those things were supposed to be safe?" said Hurley. "Even ancient wrecks like *Vengeance* protect their reactors. They're the most vulnerable part of the ship!"

"True," agreed Fernandez, "but no amount of engineering can

defend a ship against a massive attack like this. It's because of great engineering that this ship hasn't blown already. My guess is that if *Vengeance* had sustained this level of damage, she'd be a blown-up bag of nuts and bolts by now."

Hurley grunted, but whether he was agreeing with Fernandez or not was unclear. "So what do we do next?" he asked.

"We go into the containment area," said Fernandez, "and we find out exactly what's gone wrong."

"What, in there? Right next to the nukes?" Hurley sounded outraged at the prospect.

"Of course," snapped Fernandez. "How else did you think we would do this?"

"Shit!" said Hurley as Tofler floated around the reactor. "Is that why you brought us? So you'd have someone disposable to do the dirty work?"

"I brought you because I can't do this on my own," said Fernandez angrily. "You think I want to be here?"

"I'm an IT technician," said Hurley. "I didn't sign up to play around with nuclear reactors and go home with glowing red bollocks."

"The only way you'll go home with glowing red bollocks," snarled Fernandez, now properly angry, "is because I placed my boot in the middle of them due to the fact that you wouldn't do your damned job!"

Tofler had hauled himself back around the reactor, and he and Hurley floated in front of Fernandez. Neither of them seemed keen to get closer to the reactor.

"I'll do it," said York, pushing Hurley aside. "There's no radiation to speak of, and the suit will block much of the rest."

"Fine," said Fernandez. "You two monitor things from out here, we'll check the reactor. Okay?"

"Yes, sir," said Hurley, pushing away from the containment chamber to float in front of the remaining monitors.

Fernandez shook his head and moved over to the door, and peered in through the inspection panel.

York opened a private channel. "You sure about this, sir?"

"You have a better idea? Now's the time to shout."

"The main fusion reactors are down, but there's still power in the system," said York, "because reactor one, the other half of the pair, is still running."

"Powering the monitors and some of the ship's systems," said Fernandez.

"Right, and Rietveld-Muers reactors aren't really dangerous, but that crack is bad and we can't leave this one running. But what if we run a controlled power-down? Put both reactors in a standby state."

"The ship loses the last of her power," said Fernandez.

"But everything critical is either running off local backups or so badly damaged that it isn't operating anyway," said York. "And in standby, there's no chance of the reactors failing and exploding."

Fernandez was quiet for a few seconds as he thought through the implications. Then he nodded. "Fine, let's do it. Do you know how?"

"Pinging you the instruction manual now, sir," said York, "but it's not rocket science."

"Wait, did you hear that?" said Fernandez suddenly. "Like a faint tapping sound." He spun gently in mid-air, trying to find the source of the tapping over the background noise of the ship's slow death.

"No," said York as she floated over to the reactor's backup control panel and began working through the initialisation routine. "Hurley," she said, flicking back to the team's channel, "get over to that console and keep an eye on the power output levels. Tofler, there's a manual override key over there, somewhere," she said, gesturing at a control room that opened off the main chamber. "Find it and get ready."

Tofler floated across to the door and opened it. "In here?"

York looked up. "That's the main control room. Check to see if you have comms with the reactors and the outside world."

"You've done this before, York?" said Fernandez as he watched her working down the checklist.

"No, sir, this isn't something we do outside space dock," said York, "but I've done the training sims a few times. Easy."

"I'm not reassured, Midshipman," said Fernandez drily.

"It'll be fine, sir," said York as another rumble ran through the ship. "Probably," she added quietly. "Power levels?"

"Er, bouncing around a bit," said Hurley. "Somewhere around twenty percent."

"If it hits forty, shout," said York. "You found that key yet, Tofler?"

"Big red switch marked 'Emergency Stop'?"

"That's it," said York as she worked through the checklist, flicking at controls as she went. "Wait for my signal."

There was another bang that shook the ship and rattled the fixtures. "Something's still firing at us," said Fernandez as he watched the crack in the containment vessel. "Maybe *Target Six* wasn't as dead as we hoped."

"Tofler, stand by," said York. Then she paused, head cocked to one side as she listened. "Did you hear that tapping?"

"They're coming for us," said Hurley, an edge of panic in his voice. "We need to get out of here."

"Keep it together, Hurley," said Fernandez, "we're almost done."

York shouted instructions and worked at her panel, steadily moving through the process. "Almost there," she said, floating over to another panel to make an adjustment. "How's the power output?"

"Er, spiking to the high thirties," said Hurley.

"Shit," said York, darting back across the room to make more changes to the settings. "Now?"

"Low forties," said Hurley.

"What's happening, York?" said Fernandez.

"No idea, sir," said York. "Power output should be steady as we wind down. Something's wrong."

A scream echoed through the room, a drawn-out wail of anguish and pain. When it ended, the silence it left behind was cold and eerie.

"What the fuck was that?" said Tofler.

"Nothing human," said Hurley, pushing away from his station. "I told you, they're coming for us!"

"Get back to your post," snapped Fernandez.

But Hurley looked around, movements shaky and erratic. "I'm not waiting here to die," he yelled, and he pushed off the wall, heading for the door.

"Tofler, hit the switch," said York, entirely focussed on her checklist. When nothing happened, she looked up, searching for Tofler. But he was gone, out the door with Hurley and fleeing from whatever demons they feared now roamed the ship.

"Shit," said York, gesturing wildly at the control room, "hit the switch, sir, hit the switch!"

Fernandez pushed away from his station as another groaning tear pulled at the ship's fabric and shook the walls.

"Hurry, we have only seconds," said York, desperately splitting her attention between her own console and Fernandez's progress to the control room.

The lieutenant bounced off a doorframe, then hauled himself into the control room as the ship rumbled again. "Where is it?" he said in desperation, casting around for the switch.

"Behind you," said York, "on the wall, big red thing."

Fernandez spun, almost lost control. "Got it!" he said, flipping open the switch's cover. He pressed the switch. "Done," he yelled.

York pulled herself to the main console and checked the power outputs. Reactor one was powering down to standby, exactly as expected. "Power output still rising in reactor two," she muttered, confused. She flicked through the instructions again, trying to work out what had gone wrong. Then she saw it: a missed step. "Shit," she said, flicking at the panel. "Again!"

Fernandez hit the switch again, and suddenly the lights dimmed. "What's that?"

"It worked," said York with a sigh of relief. "Power output dropping, lights switching to battery backup, reactor powering down. It's done, we're safe."

"Good work," said Fernandez. He flipped open the faceplate of his helmet to let air blow across his face and looked at York. "I'll update the admiral."

Then he heard it again: the tap, tap, tap of little metallic feet on steel.

Probably nothing, he thought, *just the ship settling.* But when he turned to look out through the control room door, there was an OctoBot staring at him from the wall.

"Oh, shit," said Fernandez in a small voice.

6

"Say that again," said Ten, "and use small words."

"The console is working," said Davies, speaking with exaggerated care. "The power is connected. The computers are ready. But the comms link has been severed. At the other end."

"At the other end?" repeated Ten. He paused, waiting for Davies to explain. "What do you mean, 'the other end'?" he asked when Davies said nothing more.

"At the business end," said Davies cryptically, "where this control room links into the Sphere's central network so that commands can be relayed to the executing sub-systems."

"So we're fucked," said Conway, succinctly summarising the situation.

Davies nodded. "Looks that way," he said. "The Mechs have locked us out, so we can't take control of the Sphere."

"Knew this would happen," said Jackson. "They're damned cunning, these Mechs."

"Okay," said Ten slowly, thinking it through, "but nothing else has happened, right? The Mechs might have locked us out, but they haven't taken control of the Sphere."

"Well, no," conceded Davies, "but–"

"Okay, so we're fucked," said Ten wagging a finger, "but we're not – if I might coin a phrase – 'proper fucked', because the Mechs have fucked themselves at the same time as fucking us, and all we need to do to recover the situation is connect the one remaining control room – this one – to the rest of the fucking network." He looked around at the others. "Right?"

Davies nodded. "Something like that, yes, but–"

Ten interrupted again. "The Mechs've got the network hub, we've got the control room, and neither works without the other, right?"

"Yes," said Davies, desperately trying to finish a sentence, "but–"

"So we'd better get fucking moving," said Ten firmly, "because those bastards have been one step ahead of us all bloody day, and if we've worked out what's going on, you can be damn certain they have too."

"Right," said Davies, vigorously nodding his head, relieved that someone else had said it. "They'll pile in here and try to kill us all and capture the control room."

"Or stand off and waste us from a distance with rocket launchers and high explosives," said Jackson. The others turned to stare at him. "What?" he said innocently. "It's what I'd do if I didn't need the room!"

"Let's assume they need the room because the Sphere is important to their diabolical plan," said Conway, "and make sure they don't get it."

"They'll be coming," said Ten as he checked his weapons. "They'll all be coming."

"Of course they will," said Conway with a sigh. She opened a channel to Captain Figgis and updated him on the situation. "You'll have to keep them away from here while we fix this," she said finally.

"What the fuck do you think we're doing?" said Figgis. "Sixty minutes, that's all I can offer. After that, we'll be using blades and throwing rocks."

"Roger," said Conway. "Out." She flipped open her helmet and looked at the rest of the small team. Davies was at the console, still trying to find a way around the Mechs' comms interruption. Jackson was shuffling anxiously, glancing at the doors and checking his weapons repeatedly, as if fearing the worst. Gray was walking up and down, rifle at the ready as she turned from one door to the other, guarding everything.

But Ten was still. Quiet and calm, he seemed utterly confident and in control, unaffected by the noise and chaos. Conway shared a look with him, and the ancient Penal Marine nodded.

"One hour to save civilisation as we know it?" he said with a smirk. "Let's do this."

Conway grinned back. "Right, so here's the plan," she said firmly. "Davies stays here to do the tech stuff; if you find a better solution, great. If not, the rest of us fight our way out of here to the comms link and patch this console back into the network."

"Destroying as many Mechs as we can on the way," said Ten.

"Obviously," said Conway.

"And what happens if we don't get there? Or if the Mechs find another way to block us? Or if they break through Figgis' defence and destroy the console?" said Jackson. "Asking for a friend."

"Then we lose control of the last fighting vessel we have," said Conway. "*Vengeance* will be captured or destroyed, the Mechs will sweep through the portal, and they'll launch an unstoppable attack on Sol-controlled planets and stations. We stop them here, now, or we don't stop them at all."

"Mission failure," said Ten in a flat tone, "is not an option."

"Fair enough," said Jackson. "Better get this done, then."

While the rest of the team scavenged ammunition and other supplies, Conway took the opportunity to contact *Vengeance* and update Admiral Stansfield on the situation.

"I'm not sure I like the sound of this," said Stansfield as Conway explained. "It seems an awfully risky plan upon which to bet the farm."

"I agree, sir," said Conway emphatically, "but it's the best option we've got. If we lose control of the Sphere to the Mechs..." She trailed off without finishing the sentence; they all knew what would happen if the Mechs controlled the Sphere.

"Yes, well," said Stansfield, "when you put it like that, I suppose we'll have to take any chance we can."

"Thank you, sir. Is there any news from *Orion*?"

"Captain Ryan's evacuation continues," said Stansfield, "but he needs more time to complete the operation. Of Lieutenant Fernandez and his team, there is nothing but an ominous silence."

"Very good, sir," said Conway, not liking the thought that things might be getting worse on *Orion*. "I'll update you again as soon as we have news."

"Do that, Trooper," said Stansfield, "and good luck. Stansfield out."

"We have the old man's reluctant blessing," said Conway. "Ready?"

"Ready as I'll ever be," said Gray.

"Not as ready as I'd like to be," said Jackson despondently.

"Ready," said Ten simply, closing his helmet.

"Engineering," said Stansfield, opening a channel to *Vengeance's* depleted technical teams, "what's the situation? How long till we have engines and weapons?"

"Sub-Lieutenant Warburton here, sir," said a woman's voice. "We have teams working to restart the primary reactors, but there's a lot of damage to repair in the power-couplings, the control systems and the cooling conduits."

"An hour?" said Stansfield. "Twenty hours? Six weeks?"

"Full power will take weeks, sir," said Warburton, "but we're working to get enough power to give you manoeuvring thrusters and at least some of the railgun batteries."

"And how long will *that* take?" growled Stansfield.

"At least another couple of hours, sir," said Warburton unhappily. Giving bad news to admirals was never a career-enhancing move.

"I need the main engines, all the railgun batteries and the torpedo tubes, Warburton," said Stansfield coldly, "or our position is likely to get substantially worse."

"I understand, sir, but there's only so much we can–"

"Just get it done," snapped Stansfield. "I want a progress report in thirty minutes." He closed the channel and turned to Vernon, who was issuing orders and reviewing reports on his data slate. "Ed, what's the news?"

Vernon looked up. "It's not all bad, to be honest. *Vengeance* is back under our control and we believe we've cleared all the Mechs and OctoBots."

"Good," said Stansfield with a nod.

"Haworth has engaged *Target Six,* and although they aren't able to inflict a killer blow against a ship of that size, they do seem to have slowed the rate at which Mechs are being despatched to board *Orion* from a flood to a trickle."

Stansfield grunted. A reduction in the flow of Mechs from *Target Six* was good news, but it might simply reflect the Mechs' growing confidence in their ability to take and control *Orion.*

"That's another possible explanation," admitted Vernon when Stansfield explained his reservations, "or it could be that they've launched all their troops. Either way, it seems to put a limit on the number of Mechs that Charlie Team will need to deal with."

"Is that it?" asked Stansfield when Vernon fell silent.

The commander nodded. "I'm afraid so, sir. I'd love to have more to give you, but that's it for now. Sorry."

"Does anyone else have news?" said Stansfield, throwing the question out across the bridge.

"I do, sir," said Lieutenant Yau, and something in his tone brought a chill to the back of Stansfield's neck. Yau flicked at his console, and a grainy image flashed onto the main screen.

"What am I looking at, Lieutenant?" said Stansfield. The screen showed a patch of space filled with stars and not much else. Beautiful, in its own way, but not hugely informative or interesting.

"Here, sir," said Yau as a green circle appeared around a dim star on the display.

"It's a dull, boring star," said Stansfield. "Why do we care about it?"

"Because it's not a star, sir," said Yau. "We're lucky to see it. If she hadn't passed in front of a densely-packed nebula, we might never have noticed her, and even then, we were only looking in the right direction because the targeting computer hadn't been updated."

"Noticed who?" said Stansfield, although he had a horrible feeling that he knew exactly what they were looking at.

"It's *Target One*, sir," said Yau. "She's not dead, and it looks like she's manoeuvring for another attack run."

Vernon looked up from his data slate, attention suddenly focused on the main display.

Stansfield stared for a few seconds. "How long till she's within range?" he growled.

"Impossible to say, sir," said Yau. "What with the extreme range, the degradation to our sensors, the lack of detail about the damage she suffered and our general lack of information about her capabilities, it's very–"

"I get the picture, Lieutenant," said Stansfield. "Add *Target One* to the threat register and keep monitoring her."

"Already done, sir," said Yau. "We'll know as soon as she starts to move, although we might not be able to tell exactly what she's doing."

Stansfield snorted. "The day we know exactly what the enemy is doing is the day we finally win every encounter. Keep me informed."

"Aye, sir."

"Get an update from Lieutenant Fernandez," said Stansfield. "I want to know how long *Orion* has left."

"No response from Lieutenant Fernandez, sir," said Midshipman Campbell at the communication console. "We've had nothing from him or his team since they reached the reactor chamber."

"Then try Kearney," snapped Stansfield, "and have her find out what's going on with Fernandez. We have to know what's going on!"

"Aye, sir," said Campbell. There was a pause. "Trooper Kearney is engaged, sir. She has no information on the lieutenant, but will report in as soon as she knows more."

Stansfield took a few deep breaths. "Understood, Midshipman. Keep me informed."

"Aye, sir."

"There's one more thing, sir," said Yau. The distant image of *Target One* shrank down to a corner of the main display, replaced by a view of the portal. "Something's changed about the portal."

"The green flashes?" said Stansfield wearily. "And why is this important?"

"Er, I don't know, sir," admitted Yau, "but I thought you should know that the portal's behaviour had changed."

"Thank you, Lieutenant," said Stansfield. "The list of things we don't understand just keeps getting longer."

"They're toying with us," said Vernon. "Trying to wear us down."

"Maybe," said Stansfield as he peered at the display. "But to what end?"

And to that, nobody had any answer.

7

O*rion*'s main shuttle bay was a mess. The worst of the damage was at one end, where explosions had torn away a chunk of the deck and punched holes in the hull. The resulting windstorm, as atmosphere vented into space, had dragged everything from the deck that wasn't firmly tied down, and when the gravity had failed, the debris had floated free to drift across the bay.

There was precious little atmosphere left in this part of the ship, and none in the shuttle bays, so most of the evacuating crew wore emergency environmental protection suits. Some – mostly those who had been furthest from the initial strikes – were encased in suits of power armour, and a few even wore engineering suits.

The bay's main doors were stuck half open, wedged against the twisted ceiling. Each shuttle that entered or left, the bay was forced to edge carefully through the narrow gap, then manoeuvre across the bay to the staging point where the crew had gathered. It was perilous work.

"Keep it moving," said Lieutenant Woodhall, one hand clamped to a handle on the wall and the other waving the shocked and disoriented crew across the void to the waiting shuttles. He was still wearing the suit he'd been given on *Vengeance*, and it was starting to show its age.

"Don't stop, go straight to the shuttle marked in red in your HUD, squeeze in," said Woodhall for what felt like the hundredth time.

A private channel opened in his HUD, and a message appeared from Captain Ryan, who was searching *Orion* for survivors. <How many left?>

Woodhall looked around, estimating the numbers. <About sixty here. Next shuttle away in a few minutes>

<Is Fernandez with you?>

Woodhall hesitated, frowning inside his helmet. Why would Ryan be asking about Fernandez? <No. Isn't he with you?>

<No sign of him, and no news. Investigating. Out>

The channel closed before Woodhall could ask any further questions. "Strange," he muttered.

Ryan was deep in the ship with his small team of Marines. They had a case of emergency environmental suits and were searching for any remaining survivors, hunting through wrecked rooms and corridors to find crew members who might still be alive. They'd rescued several people, all injured to some degree or other, and sent them off to the main bay for evacuation. Now, though, they were finding only bodies.

"Another," said Corporal Adams as they cleared a room. The hull had been quickly breached near here, and many people had been caught by the sudden depressurisation. "Poor buggers never stood a chance."

Ryan grunted at the implied criticism. Outwardly, the three Marines were respectful and obedient, but he could feel their disgust. This was his failure, and he hadn't even been here to share the crew's risks.

"Next room," he said, gesturing along the corridor. He pushed away from bulkhead and floated towards the next room, using his hands to arrest his motion when he reached the door.

The Marines hadn't moved. Marine Varo was staring the other way, and Martinez-Gonzalez – universally known as Emgee – was fiddling with his weapon. All three Marines floated where Ryan had left them, next to the previous room.

"Are you coming?" he said angrily. The last thing he needed was an argument with the Marines, but he wasn't about to put up with tardiness or disobedience.

"Is there anything more we can do, sir?" said Adams. "We haven't found a survivor for thirty-five minutes, and this part of the ship is getting pretty cold."

"We're not leaving till we've searched every room," snapped Ryan, "and found every person still alive on the ship."

There was an uncomfortable shifting amongst the Marines, who clearly weren't keen to continue the search.

"I think we've found them all, sir," said Adams. "Maybe we should get the backup devices, the Mind State Protection systems, and get away ourselves?"

"Move," said Ryan, "that's an order!"

The Marines hesitated, looking to Adams for guidance.

"This is damned close to mutiny, Corporal," said Ryan darkly, "and I won't hesitate to throw the book at you."

"Sorry, sir," said Adams, "but I think things have changed." He pointed past the captain along the corridor.

Ryan turned, flipping easily in the zero-G to face the other way. At the far end of the corridor, a pair of Marines was approaching, barrelling along as quickly as they could go. They came to a sudden halt when they saw Captain Ryan, locking themselves to the corridor walls and raising their rifles. Behind them were more figures. More Marines, Ryan realised, all wearing the standard dark grey power armour like the three on his team.

A channel request appeared in Ryan's HUD and he accepted it without thinking about it, so surprised was he to meet up with such a large group of survivors.

"Captain Ryan?" said the voice.

"Obviously," replied Ryan. His pale grey power armour made him stand out from the dark-clad Marines, with his insignia of rank and standing emblazoned in bright colours on his chest. The contrast to the Marine who floated in front of him, his armour battered and scarred, couldn't have been plainer. "Who are you?" said Ryan, hunting for the Marine's name and rank.

"Trooper Hunter, Penal Marine, sir," said Hunter. "Pleased to meet you, but we need to go. This area isn't safe."

"The Penal Marine?" snapped Ryan, disgust evident in his voice. Stansfield had mentioned a Penal Marine, but he had assumed the man was raving under the pressures of his failed command. If he had realised he was serious, he would have taken action.

"You can thank me later, sir," said Hunter, utterly unflustered by Ryan's hostility, "but right now we need to move." He paused, then gestured back along the corridor when Ryan remained still. "That way, in case I wasn't clear."

"You'll come with me, Marine," snapped Ryan, "and help with the search. We don't leave till–"

"Begging your pardon, sir," said Hunter with just a hint of threat, "but me and the lads'll be moving along now. The only things alive back there" – he jerked his thumb over his shoulder – "are Mechs, and they're coming this way."

From along the corridor, two more Marines appeared, the last of Hunter's team. They moved quickly, one moving hand over hand along the wall, the other floating backwards, attached to a cable and towed by his colleague. The second Marine's rifle pointed back along the corridor.

Something happened with his HUD, and Ryan was pulled into the Marines' chaotic team channel.

"They're right behind us," said Petticrew, looking around. "Why have we stopped?"

Behind Petticrew, the last member of Hunter's team – Ogilvie – turned to see what was happening. She unclipped her cable and wedged her foot against a bulkhead, then turned her attention back to the shadowy section at the end of the corridor.

"Orders, Captain?" said Corporal Adams.

Ryan looked from Adams to Hunter. "Nobody left alive?" he asked in a hushed voice.

"No, sir," said Hunter, almost feeling sorry for the captain, "nobody at all."

"Then let's go," Ryan said after a pause.

"Roger," said Adams, turning around. He pulled himself along the corridor, heading back the way they had come. "Shit!" he said suddenly, scrabbling for his rifle.

Ogilvie brought her weapon to bear as gunfire flashed. New holes were punched in the walls and the Marines took cover, pulling themselves into the minimal protection of the rooms that lined the corridor.

"Mechs," said Ogilvie unnecessarily. "Looks like they crept past us."

Adams spun as the rounds caught his shoulder, twisting him around so that he struggled to face the enemy. Then he yelled as his armour failed and a bullet tore into his leg.

"Corp!" said Marine Varo, grabbing Adams' foot and hauling him to the side of the corridor. "Keep breathing!"

"The thought had bloody occurred to me," snapped Adams through the pain.

Emgee pulled a can from his pack and sprayed the hole in Adams' armour. The liquid turned immediately to foam, filling the gap in the armour and plugging the wound to stop the bleeding. Adams groaned a little, but at least the flesh of his leg was no longer exposed to the chill of space.

Ogilvie fired from cover, paused, then fired again. In the vacuum, the muzzle flare was startlingly bright, but the absence of noise made the whole thing seem unreal.

"You'll be okay, Corp," said Emgee, interfacing with Adams' medical readouts. He ordered a round of synthetic opioids for the corporal and watched as the suit dispensed them. "Good to go," he said as the drugs took effect and Adams' heart rate began to fall back towards normal.

"Keep moving," ordered Hunter, firing down the corridor then pushing off from the doorway towards the Mechs, firing as he went.

Ryan had a pistol in his hand, but he seemed unsure what to do with it. Hunter let go of his rifle to grab the captain by his arms. "Stick with us, sir," he said, hauling the officer along and pushing him across the junction. If Ryan objected to being manhandled, he showed no sign.

"They're still behind us," said Petticrew. "Firing again." More muzzle flashes, and now the team faced Mechs at both ends of the corridor.

"Shit," said Hunter as two more Mechs appeared right in front of him. He fired, killing one and colliding with the other. Then he was on top of them, punching out with his cybernetic arm. His fist smashed into the creature's face, and he felt bone crunch beneath his blows.

"Time to get to the shuttles," he yelled, pushing the corpse away and bringing his rifle around. He shot a third Mech to clear the way. "Move," he yelled, pulling his people along the corridor and across the junction where the Mechs had appeared. Petticrew was firing again, floating up the corridor as the Mechs gathered just out of sight at the far end.

"Time to go," said Petticrew. He and Ogilvie were taking turns to fire on the Mechs, then retreat a few metres, running a sort of zero-G retreat equivalent of the bounded overwatch. It worked as a rearguard action, but it was slow.

"Faster," said Hunter, firing past Ogilvie as she pulled herself another couple of metres towards the relative safety of the junction. "Forget it," he said as Ogilvie turned, looking for another firing position, "just get over here."

"Roger," said Ogilvie, pushing hard to skim past Hunter and through the open doorway.

Hunter fired again, covering Petticrew's retreat as he pushed through the junction. He was almost across when something large and grey cannoned through the junction and smashed into Petticrew. The Marine yelled in surprise as the impact carried him away from the team.

"What the hell was that?" said Hunter, still firing at the Mechs that were now making their way cautiously towards them.

"Help!" said Petticrew. "Help, argh!"

Hunter made a move to go after Petticrew, but as soon as he emerged from cover, a fusillade of enemy fire forced him back. Ogilvie tried from the other side of the corridor, but Hunter caught her and pulled her back.

There was another yell from Petticrew. Hunter could only watch the readouts in his HUD as Petticrew was carried further away, his heart rate spiking. Then the indicator went red. Petticrew was dead.

8

OctoBots never travelled alone. York had learned that lesson the hard way as she and Fernandez had fought their way out of the reactor chamber with the two Marines, Muller, and Douglas.

"Got my eye in now," said Douglas as she shot another OctoBot, blasting it out of mid-air as it leapt across the room.

"Easy with that beast," grumbled Muller, whose standard-issue rifle looked almost like a toy alongside Douglas' combat shotgun. "Spray and pray, right?"

"You're just jealous," said Douglas as she shot another OctoBot. She looked around to where Lieutenant Fernandez and Midshipman York were working to open the next door. "Better not keep them waiting."

Muller grunted and switched back to the team channel.

York was muttering something as she jammed her crowbar into the doorframe and heaved, using the suit's strength to lever the door open. Contrary to York's understanding of the regulations, some of *Orion*'s doors lacked battery backup, and powering down the reactors had been enough to lock them closed.

"Gotcha," she muttered as her lever overcame the resistance of the door's mechanism. She stuck her head out and checked for movement before pulling herself into the room beyond.

"Clear," she said, turning back to watch the Marines as Fernandez floated past. He had a pistol in his hand, but against the OctoBots his shooting was proving less effective than the York's crowbar.

Muller pulled himself into the new room and headed for the next door. That's what this mission had become: a never-ending sequence of doors, rooms and corridors as they attempted to fight their way back to the shuttle bay.

Fernandez trailed after Muller, desperately trying to face both forwards to see where he was going and back to see what was following. He banged into the wall and halted, pistol aimed across the room.

"Might as well put it away, sir," said Muller, who was peering through the small reinforced panel in the door into the corridor beyond. "More chance of hitting your foot than the enemy."

"Thank you, Muller," said Fernandez coldly. "I'll have you know I was a champion shot with a pistol when I first joined up."

"Ah, that'll be it then, sir," said Muller, heaving on the door handle to no obvious effect. "The clone you're wearing now's probably faulty."

Fernandez was prevented from answering by an incoming message.

"Fernandez," said the voice, "this is Yau. If you can hear me, the Mechs are placing mines on *Orion*'s hull. No idea why, but there's a secondary rendezvous point that'll keep you away from the danger area. If you see Captain Ryan or Troopers Kearney, Mason or Hunter, let them know that the main bay is no longer safe. Good luck. Yau out."

Fernandez tried to reply, but the message was a recording, not a conversation, and when he tried to ping *Vengeance* he got no response. He pulled up the new rendezvous point and checked it against their current position, then pinged the details to York. "New plan," he said. "Can we get to this bay?"

York was quiet for a few moments as she checked the location of the bay on her plans. "Shit," she said finally. "Maybe, but the quickest route is back that way," she said, pointing back at the room they'd just left.

"Back?" said Douglas as she watched for OctoBots from the doorway. "You're kidding, right?"

Then Muller reared back from the observation panel in the door as something flashed past. "What the hell was that?"

"What?" said Fernandez, distracted.

"There's something out there," said Muller, "something big and fast."

"Rubbish," snapped Fernandez. "There are OctoBots and probably Mechs, nothing else."

Something slammed up against the door, making it judder in its frame. Muller looked out, then quickly slid away. "It's a Mech," he said, "a big one. Huge. It's pounding on the door."

"Not that way, then," said Fernandez. And that left only one option: the lift shaft in the corner of the room.

York floated over and levered open the doors. The lift was three decks down. "This'll work," she said, wedging the doors open. She looked at Muller, then blinked as the door he floated beside bulged under the force of a blow. "Come on, move!" she said, waving.

"Yeah, good idea," said Muller, pushing away from his buckling door and floating backwards towards the lift shaft.

Lieutenant Fernandez took another look at the door, then followed Muller.

"Douglas, move," said Muller as the door began to give way. Douglas looked around and saw the danger. She squeezed off another round, then floated away from her door, heading for the lift.

Then the second door failed completely, battered from its frame by the huge armoured Mech. Door and Mech burst into the room, carried forward by the creature's huge momentum.

Douglas spun as she crossed the room and fired at the Mech. For all the effect she had, she might as well have sworn at the thing. Fernandez and Muller joined in, emptying their magazines into the thing. The Mech waved its arms and floated away under the impact of the rounds, but it wasn't clear how badly hurt it might be, if at all.

"Go," said Fernandez, grabbing at Douglas and yanking her towards the lift shaft. He forced her through the doorway as she protested, then turned back for Muller. The second Marine had reloaded his rifle and was carefully drilling rounds into the Mech, probing for weak points in the thing's armour.

"Muller, let's go," said Fernandez. "That's an order!"

"Coming," said Muller, pulling his foot from its lock on the wall and pushing away so that he floated towards the lift shaft. He fired again, aiming at the Mech's knee as it drifted away, arms flailing.

The Mech smacked into the far wall and steadied itself. It bunched its legs under its body and launched itself at Muller, arms outstretched.

"Shit," said Muller as the thing flew across the room at speed. He switched modes on his rifle and fired full-auto at the Mech's head as it came toward him. At the last moment, he twisted so that the Mech's flight caught him on the shoulder and carried him back against the wall.

"Muller," said Fernandez, reloading his pistol as fast as he could.

The Mech had ripped away Muller's rifle, and now seemed intent on removing the Marine's arm. Muller screamed and pounded at the Mech with his free hand, but to no avail.

Then Douglas appeared. She ducked under Muller's arm to ram the end of her shotgun into the joint between the Mech's chin and its neck.

"Argh!" she yelled as she squeezed the trigger. Pellets from the first round ricocheted off the armour and bounced around the room, pinging off Douglas's arm, but she kept firing, and the second round burst through the Mech's armour.

After three more rounds, Muller put his hand on her arm. "It's dead, Douglas," he said quietly.

Douglas stopped firing and pulled her shotgun away, breathing hard. The Mech floated free, tumbling slowly away when Muller prodded it. "Yup," he said, "you nailed it."

"Difficult to miss at that range," said Douglas quietly.

"Even the lieutenant would have been able to hit that thing," said Muller, pulling Douglas towards the lift shaft, "but now we need to move again."

"Yeah, right," said Douglas distractedly, still staring at the corpse of the huge Mech.

Movement at the door frame signalled the arrival of the first Octo-Bot. The thing eased its way cautiously into the room and sat on the wall, staring at the two Marines.

"Need to reload," said Douglas as Muller hauled her into the lift shaft. A second OctoBot crawled into the room, then a third.

"Two decks down," said York, "and don't forget to close the door."

Douglas slammed a new magazine into her shotgun, but before she could bring it to bear on the OctoBots, Muller knocked away the wedge and heaved the door shut. The room disappeared from view, leaving the two Marines in the very dark lift shaft.

"Cosy," said Douglas.

"Go," said Muller, pulling himself down the shaft towards the light from Fernandez's helmet lamps.

Douglas watched for a moment, then looked back at the lift doors, which were shaking as if something were trying to open them. "Not a good place to be," she muttered, quickly following the others.

Everything had gone bad almost as soon as Kearney had parted ways with Lieutenant Fernandez. She and Mason had led their teams no more than fifty metres across *Orion* in their hunt for the Mechs when they'd run straight into them. One moment, they were crossing a crew mess with no sign of the enemy, floating near the ceiling as they headed for the doors on the far side of the room, and the next they were in the middle of a firefight.

"Mechs," Leman had yelled, and then there were bullets flying everywhere as the two sides opened fire.

It seemed that the Mechs had been as surprised as the Marines –

a sort of inadvertent mutual ambush – and both sides were happy to retreat back the way they had come. Since then, they'd played a cautious game of cat and mouse as the two forces sought to trap each other and inflict a decisive blow.

"This is pointless," said Mason during a lull in the action. The Marines were ranged across some sort of engineering workshop, with doors in all four walls and a huge lift that descended to the loading bays below. "They're too savvy to fall for an ambush, and not smart enough to trap us," he said. "We've been on this bloody ship for forty minutes, and all we've done is use up our ammo."

"Agreed," said Kearney. About all they'd proven since the initial encounter was that their power armour was tougher than whatever the Mechs wore, since the casualties so far had been entirely one-sided. They all knew that couldn't last.

"So we head for the rendezvous?" said Mason hopefully.

"Yes, we're achieving nothing here," said Kearney.

"Great," said Mason. "Move out," he ordered, sharing the route to the rendezvous with the team and heading for the door.

"Hunter, you out there?" said Kearney, opening a new channel.

"Good to hear your voice," said Hunter.

"We're heading for the rendezvous point," said Kearney. "Nothing more we can do here."

"Roger, us too, with only a small detour to collect the MSP backups."

"Shit, seriously?" said Kearney as her team moved swiftly through a deserted hallway. "What happened to the remote link?"

"Buggered like the rest of this ship," said Hunter. "We'll be there in two minutes, then at the shuttles in ten."

"Roger, see you there."

"And Kearney? Watch out for some new variant of Mech. Huge fuckers, heavily armoured. We've seen a couple, and they're as hard as nails."

"Great," muttered Kearney, "just what we need. Laters." She cut the channel and looked at Mason, who shrugged. There was nothing left for them to do but flee.

9

"What's going on out there?" said Ten on the command channel. Captain Figgis had reluctantly brought Conway into the channel to facilitate cooperation between Charlie Team and his Marines, but he'd categorically refused to allow Ten to listen in.

That hadn't stopped Conway pulling Ten into the channel as soon as Figgis' metaphorical back was turned, but she hadn't really expected him to speak.

"Too late now," she muttered as she listened to the officers of Figgis' company asking why there was a Penal Marine on their command channel.

"We have a plan," said Conway, cutting across the chatter. As Charlie Team's lead, she had enough standing for them to at least listen. She outlined the plan. "So we need a perimeter around Davies and the control room, and then a managed retreat to the shuttles."

"This sounds damned risky," said Figgis. "I don't like it. If we don't have control of the Sphere, we should just leave while we can."

"Run if you want," said Ten, "but you can't hide from this one, Figgis."

Conway rolled her eyes and slapped Ten's shoulder. Baiting Figgis wasn't going to help.

"The only way out is through, sir," said Conway while Figgis was still struggling to form a coherent response to Ten's insubordination, "and this is our best option."

"And we've got the difficult job," said Ten. "Even you should be able to manage a simple perimeter defence."

Conway clenched her fists, seriously considering shooting Ten. "We'll keep you updated," she said through gritted teeth. "Out." She muted the channel and turned to Ten. "What the hell was that about? This is a team game, Ten! We need Figgis to get the job done."

Ten shrugged and Conway stared, open-mouthed. He'd been different ever since Figgis had come aboard. He'd always been awkward, but now he'd crossed a line and was making life really difficult.

"Are we going?" said Jackson, unaware of the tensions on the command channel. "Only we're on the clock, and we've got a job to do."

"Move out," said Conway, with a glance at Ten. He hadn't said anything, but she could almost feel the anger boiling off his suit. "Stairs and up, quiet as we can."

Ten was first through the door, leading the way and moving smoothly onto the stairs. Jackson and Gray followed, leaving Conway to take the rear-guard.

She looked back at Davies from the doorway. "You going to be okay, Double-D?"

"Sure," said Davies, not looking up from his work. "Just gotta get this thing working, stop an alien invasion, save *Vengeance*, and escape a wrecked enemy starship. Piece of cake."

"Focus, Davis," said Conway firmly. He looked up and nodded. "One thing at a time."

"Got it, boss," said Davies. "You can count on me."

"Good," said Conway, "because that means I only have to worry about Ten." She closed the channel before Davies could respond, and hurried after Jackson and Gray.

Flight Lieutenant Haworth and his modest squadron were holding position between *Vengeance* and *Orion*, ostensibly screening the evacuation effort from the enemy but, in reality, merely holding station and waiting for something to happen. It was staggeringly dull.

"Anyone see anything of interest?" he asked. The squadron duly reported, each pilot confirming in turn that nothing of note had happened.

"Haworth, this is Vernon," said a new voice as the last report came in. Haworth blinked, suddenly awake to the possibility of action.

"Haworth here, sir. All quiet, as far as we can tell."

"Well, it's not quiet over here, Lieutenant," said Vernon. "*Target One* is still alive. Stay alert for anything that might indicate her intentions."

"Roger," said Haworth. *That* was news, albeit most unwelcome. "The evacuation seems to be going well, sir," he said, mostly to have something to say.

"Keep your eyes on *Target One* and that Battle Sphere, Lieutenant," snapped Vernon, "and let me worry about the evacuation. Vernon out."

"Right you are," said Haworth to himself. He flicked at his controls to bring up a feed of the Battle Sphere, and stared at it for a few moments. It didn't seem to be doing much of anything. Electromagnetic radiation was almost non-existent, suggesting it was running on very little power. "Probably all but dead," muttered Haworth.

But something was happening on the side of the Sphere that faced *Orion*. Hidden from *Vengeance*'s view by the bulk of the Sphere, there was movement. Haworth zoomed in, blowing the image up until a small section of the Sphere's hull filled his screen.

And there it was. An open bay door. A small one, certainly, but open nonetheless.

"You sneaky little buggers," whispered Haworth. He zoomed

further in, pushing the camera to its limits, and watched as shapes flitted out of the open door.

"*Vengeance*," he said opening a channel and sharing the feed from his ship's sensors, "this is Haworth. Take a look at this and let me know what you think."

"This is Vernon," came the reply. There was a pause, then, "That looks like Mechs leaving the Battle Sphere and heading across open space towards *Orion*."

"Yes," said Haworth, "that's what I thought. I think we might buzz past and take a closer look, if that's okay with you, *Vengeance*?"

"By all means, Lieutenant," said Commander Vernon. "Fire at will. Vernon out."

"Poor old Will," muttered Haworth, mouthing the aeons-old joke like a mantra. He updated the orders for his team. "Away we go," he said to himself, turning his ship to point toward the Mechs and engaging the targeting computer.

He took three deep breaths, calming himself as he always did before action; then he gave the order to attack and hit the trigger for the main engines. The tiny ship roared away, closing the distance to the Mechs in less than a minute, and Haworth whooped with delight for the sheer joy of the fight.

He couldn't recall an encounter quite like this. Never in his wildest dreams had he thought to see three immobilised capital ships so close together that a brave person might spacewalk between them. In all his years in space, he'd never been able to play a role quite like this in battle. It was exhilarating!

Half his squadron came with him, tearing through the void, accelerating as hard as their specialised clones would allow. Ahead, the cloud of Mechs resolved into individuals, all mounted on the strange disc-things that they seemed to use for personal transport.

"Enemy confirmed," said Haworth for the log, "targets identified, firing now." The computer took over, selecting the targets and firing the six railgun batteries faster than Haworth could follow. The dark shape of the Battle Sphere flashed past and then the encounter was over and he was through, clear of the Mechs and back in open space.

"No enemy fire," he said, checking his monitors. It looked like all the ships had made it through, leaving behind only a field of enemy casualties. Haworth shook his head, astonished. He'd never seen anything like it.

He opened a channel to the squadron. "Nicely done, everybody. Time for one more pass on our way back to station, I think."

As the auto-pilot manoeuvred the ship and began the main engine burn to take them back to their starting point, Haworth reviewed the targets the computer had fired upon. Most were Mechs travelling from the Battle Sphere to *Orion*, but he was intrigued to see that the AI had also used one railgun to strafe the Sphere's bay through the open door.

"Let's give that open bay a gentle tickle," he said to his team, "and see if we can just nudge things our way. Fifty percent at the bay, the rest at the Mechs, I think."

He waited for confirmation that the squadron had understood; then he gave the order for the return pass. "And good luck." They'd need it; the chances of making a second pass without casualties was as close to zero as made no difference, but Haworth had a feeling that this was the moment to push his luck.

"Haworth, what's going on?" said Vernon.

"It's like shooting fish in a barrel, sir," said Haworth as he checked the flight plan the computer had created. "We'll be back on station in less than a hundred seconds."

"You're making another run?" Vernon's tone said everything about his feelings on the soundness of the plan.

"The Battle Sphere's still showing next to no signs of activity," said Haworth, "and I think now's the time to inflict some real pain on the enemy."

"Take care, Lieutenant," warned Vernon. "These Mechs are damned tricky, and they learn fast."

"Roger," said Haworth, although he didn't really take Vernon's concerns seriously. "Starting our run in ten seconds." He punched the trigger to give the flight and targeting computers control of the vessel, then sat back to watch the action. For a moment he looked out at the huge enemy vessel that hung against the stars like a great carbuncle. There were Marines in there, scores of them, and he shuddered at the idea of being enclosed in so much hostile steel. Then the counter hit zero and the engines fired, pushing his tiny craft back towards *Vengeance* and the relative safety of the rest of the squadron.

The railgun batteries began firing almost immediately, targeting both the few Mechs still in open space and the bay beyond the Sphere's open doors. This was what flying was about for Haworth – the execution of a well-structured flight programme, and the rapid annihilation of the targets.

But his wasn't the only vessel in motion. As he flashed past the open doors and his railguns riddled the visible interior of the Sphere, a dozen Mechs on discs charged from the bay.

Haworth ducked involuntarily as a Mech passed within a metre of his ship. "Bloody close," he murmured as his railgun batteries finally powered down and the flight computer began firing the manoeuvring thrusters to take the ship back to its starting point.

As his view swung around, Haworth just had time to see a Mech collide with the last ship to make the run. Taylor's vessel, still firing as it shot past the Sphere less than a hundred metres from her hull, was struck on the rear upper section by a Mech and its disc.

A solid blow, at high speed. The force shattered the Mech, killing it instantly and pivoting Taylor's ship so that the nose pointed in a new direction. Before pilot or computer could react, the burn of the main engines had driven the vessel against the Sphere's hull.

The Sphere seemed to shudder as Taylor's vessel tore into her hull, cracking apart under the force of the impact, then bouncing away into space. It was over before Haworth had time to draw breath, and then all that was left of Taylor was a rapidly expanding shell of debris.

"You sure this is the right way, Davies?" said Ten as he squirmed his way down a narrow passage. There was barely enough room to move, and the armour wasn't making things any easier.

"Of course I'm not bloody sure," snapped Davies. "I'm working from plans created by an incomplete drone flyby."

"Okay, okay," said Ten, "it's not all fun and games down here either, you know?"

"Can it," said Conway sharply, "and keep moving. How far now?"

"What, you too?" said Davies.

"Best guess, Double-D, best guess," said Conway, taking a deep breath to calm her temper.

"Maybe fifty metres," said Davies, "then you'll open out into some sort of central chamber, and then–" He paused as a shudder ran through the Sphere. "What the hell was that?"

"No idea," snapped Ten. "You want me to take a look?" The strain was getting to all of them.

"A central chamber," Conway prompted to divert the argument.

"Right," said Davies. "And I'm guessing there'll be a port of some sort that you can plug the network link into."

"You're guessing?" said Conway, no longer quite able to contain herself.

"Yes," said Davies angrily, "I'm bloody guessing because we're trying to hack an alien starship! Anytime you think you can do a better job, feel free to fucking try!"

The channel went quiet as the team focused on working their way along the passageway, and a few minutes later Ten crouched down and squeezed along the last few metres into a room just big enough for a small team of Marines.

"Well, that's not good," he said as he peered through a grille into the central chamber. "That's not good at all."

10

"Are you fucking kidding me?" said Mason as his frustration boiled over. Their route to the evacuation point in the main bay was blocked at every turn, either by *Orion*'s continued collapse or by the Mechs, who seemed intent on making life difficult for the Marines.

"Back," said Kearney wearily, "and next left. Move, people, we're on a tight schedule."

As if to emphasise her point, *Orion* gave a little grumble. Her walls shook as something else went wrong somewhere in her superstructure.

"How much more of this can she take?" asked Marine Crank, who was wedged against a bulkhead to watch for Mechs and cover the retreat.

"Not much, at a guess," said Kearney, "so let's keep moving."

The HUD AI plotted a new route, taking into account the updated damage reports, and the team moved off again, heading outward and aft whenever they could. It would have been slow going even without the Mechs, but every junction and room had to be checked and cleared as they went.

"It'd be faster to breach the hull and flap our way back to *Vengeance*," said Marine Leman at one point.

Kearney was severely tempted to give it a go, but the risk of missing *Vengeance* and floating off into the void was just too great.

"Contact," said Stewart, ducking back at a junction. He paused for a count of three, then stuck his rifle around the corner and eased his head out to squeeze off a couple of shots. "Shit," he said, jerking back quickly. "Loads of 'em."

"Grenades," said Mason, hurling a couple of bomblets around the corner so that they bumped and tumbled along the corridor. He counted down the fuse, then waited till the flow of shrapnel and Mech-parts had passed. "Go, go, go," he said, pushing out into the junction and firing along the corridor.

Stewart followed, squeezing off a few rounds as he crossed to the relative safety of the space beyond, where Mason hauled him into cover. The rest of the team followed, but the Mechs had vanished.

"Not sure which is worse," said Kearney as she watched Stewart and Crank taking the lead and clearing a chamber. "The surprise attacks, or the sudden disappearances. I mean, where the hell have they all gone?"

"Just keep moving," said Mason. "There'll be time for introspection and philosophical questions when we're clear of this bastard hulk."

"Promise?" said Kearney quietly.

Mason looked at her, worried. "You okay?"

Kearney shook herself. "Yeah, fine," she said distractedly, "just don't see how we get out of this."

"Come on," said Mason, "it's not that bad."

"Seriously? If the Mechs don't get us, Ryan's incompetence will," she said. "Or maybe *Orion*'ll just fall apart before we get to the shuttles."

Mason frowned inside his helmet. It wasn't like Kearney to be fatalistic, but it had been a trying few days. "You'll feel better when you've shot something," he said. "And don't worry, something'll turn up pretty soon."

"You're a good friend, Mason, you know that?"

Mason wasn't sure what to say to that, but further opportunities for embarrassing personal relationship stuff were curtailed as a new channel opened in their HUDs.

"Anyone from Charlie Team hearing this?" said Hunter.

"Hunter," said Mason, "am I glad to hear your voice. Where are you?" The two teams swapped locations. "Looks like you're one deck above us and about thirty metres ahead. What are the chances, right?"

"Yeah, fab," said Hunter. "Get your arse up here and save ours, will you? We're pinned down and could do with a hand."

"What? You're asking for our help?" said Mason with mock bemusement. "Whatever next?"

"Stop fucking around and get up here," snapped Hunter. "We're taking casualties while you're playing silly buggers!"

"Roger that," said Mason, all hint of frivolity ripped away. "On our way."

"We're lost, aren't we, Midshipman?" said Lieutenant Fernandez.

"Of course not," snapped York in annoyance before adding a surly, "sir. It's just that I can't be sure which areas of the ship are passable." *Orion's* shudders seemed to have quietened down, but major damage had been done to the battleship, and crossing some parts was simply impossible.

Ahead, Douglas had paused to peer around a corner. She waved them on, then drifted across the junction.

"Next door on the right-hand wall should be cloning bay number two," said York, "and we can cut through to the elevators and go up a deck."

"Roger," said Douglas as she floated up the corridor. She stopped outside a door, peered through the inspection window and frowned. "Doesn't look much like a cloning bay," she said as she triggered the controls. "Hmm, busted," she muttered as the door remained solidly closed. She found the manual override and cranked the door open, then slid inside.

York followed, but stopped just inside the door. "This isn't the cloning bay," she said, pulling up *Orion's* plans, "looks more like the post-deployment de-brief suite. Yeah, my mistake. The other right-hand, sorry."

"What's all this stuff?" asked York, waving a hand at the icy droplets that floated around the room.

"Frozen blood," said Muller, glancing around and then moving back to the door. York jerked back from the drops she'd been inspecting. "Seen it before when someone bleeds in a vacuum."

"I think I'm going to be sick," said York.

"Can't advise it," said Muller, "but we should probably get moving."

"Hold on," said Fernandez, pointing across the room before the team could move back into the corridor. "Could that be a survivor?"

The room was set out as part classroom, part gymnasium, part food station. Amongst the resistance training machines arrayed along the far wall, there seemed to be an armoured body.

"I'll take a look, shall I?" said Douglas, already pushing off from the wall to float across the room. Muller held back, watching the corridor for signs of movement.

Douglas reached the body and turned it over. "Shit," she said, recoiling. "It's Tofler."

"Alive?" said Fernandez, although there was no obvious reason why Tofler would be lurking under a seated leg press.

"No," said Douglas. "Living people have more limbs, and Tofler's missing an arm and a leg."

"Shit," said Fernandez. "Any idea how it happened?"

Douglas glanced at the lieutenant, then looked back at Tofler's corpse, leaning close to inspect the frozen wounds. "I'm no expert, but it looks like something literally ripped the limbs out of their sockets. Death by shock, exsanguination or sheer embarrassment."

There was silence for a few seconds; then Douglas moved away to look at something else. "And here's Hurley," she said, pulling another corpse from under a table. Hurley's body floated free, turning gently in the middle of the room. "Something's chewed on his leg," she said, pointing to the thighs, where the armour had been ripped away and the flesh stripped to the bone.

"What the hell did that?" said Fernandez, unable to drag his gaze from the horror. Bits of frozen flesh were still stuck to the bone.

"Some sort of large rodent?" said Muller. The others stared at him. "Too soon?"

"Leave them," said Fernandez. "There's nothing we can do here."

"Were they backed up?" said Douglas, reluctant to leave anyone behind.

"Yes," said York, "they were part of the team sent to *Vengeance*."

"Ironic they should come all the way back here to die," said Muller.

"Let's focus on staying alive and avoiding whatever killed Tofler and Hurley," said Fernandez.

"Must be some sort of Mech," said Douglas, "right?"

"Agreed," said Fernandez, "unless enormously strong beings normally roam *Orion*'s lower halls looking for victims?"

"Not that I've heard, sir," said York as the small team moved out, "but it's been a strange couple of days."

They pieced together a plan as they went. Hunter and his team had been caught in a large room that opened off a long corridor. The Mechs held both ends of the corridor, trapping the Marines in their room, and the situation had rapidly devolved into a hideous stalemate. The Marines couldn't escape into the corridor without facing overwhelming fire from two directions, but the Mechs couldn't get close enough to the room to land a killing blow.

"How long, Kearney?" said Hunter. The situation in the room was growing desperate, and they all knew it was only a matter of time before the Mechs found a way to break through.

"Almost there," said Kearney, "but it ain't so easy back here, you know? We'll do no good if we tip our hand to the Mechs."

"We're on the right deck," said Mason. "Coming in from starboard, fifty metres, two junctions away."

"Roger," said Hunter, "give me the signal and we'll hit them from this side." He gave rapid orders to his team, repositioning them to take advantage of the imminent assault. "You might want to hang back, Captain," he said to Ryan. "This could get a bit messy."

Ryan, armed with a captured Mech rifle he clearly wasn't comfortable using, gave a curt nod. He'd stood with the Marines as they'd faced down the Mechs, but this sort of coordinated assault was well outside his training and experience.

"Coming in," said Kearney, "On three – shit, go, go, go,"

"Go, go, go," said Hunter, repeating Kearney's command and pushing himself towards the corridor, rifle up. Behind him, at the other end of the room, the Marines were already firing on the Mechs that had been pushing in from *Orion's* port side.

Hunter shot one Mech in the head, then a second in the chest. Then a round pinged off his pauldron and spun him around, throwing off his aim. He caught his foot on a bulkhead and awkwardly swung himself back, firing as he came. He couldn't see Kearney or Mason, but the Mechs were certainly distracted.

"Come on," he roared, holding his finger on the trigger to spray rounds indiscriminately into the corridor.

It wasn't enough. The Mechs absorbed his punishing fire and returned their own, hosing the corridor and Hunter's armour with bullets. He reeled back, knocked off balance and losing his grip on the bulkhead. He flailed wildly with his arms, trying to grab hold of anything he could use to pull himself back into cover, but he had floated out into the corridor, and all he could do was wait.

But the Mechs weren't waiting. Taking fire from two directions, they responded by retreating towards Hunter's room, fleeing Mason and Kearney's heavy assault. And they were shooting as they came, moving fast towards Hunter's former position.

"Shit, shit, shit," said Hunter, swinging his arms to try to bring his rifle to bear. Too slow. The Mechs boiled down the corridor ahead of Kearney's advance, and suddenly a multitude of rounds pinged off Hunter's armour, knocking him back and spinning him around again. He clattered into a surface and tried to turn to face his attackers, but the fire was relentless. His armour was solid, but it was only a matter of time before it failed.

Then the rattle of bullets against armour stopped, and Hunter was able to move freely again. He turned, rifle swinging up, only to find that the Mechs were all floating free, dead.

"What the...?" he muttered. And then he saw Captain Ryan, braced against the wall and almost lost in a haze of shell casings from his stolen weapon.

"They all just sort of floated out in front of me," said Ryan weakly, waving at the Mechs. "It seemed the right thing to do."

"Works for me," said Hunter, spinning around to check behind him. Marines Ogilvie and Egan were wedged against the walls of the corridor, while Hamilton and Sergeant Rodha checked for survivors amongst the Mechs.

"All dead," Hamilton reported a few seconds later. "There's only four corpses. I'd expected there to be shitloads of them."

"Seemed like more when the bastards were shooting at us," muttered Ogilvie.

Kearney and Mason floated down from the starboard corridor.

"Good work, Hunter," said Mason. "Couldn't have done it without a bloody great bullet magnet to soak up their fire like that. Nice."

"Fuck off," said Hunter, "it was all part of the plan."

"Yeah, right," said Kearney.

"So can we go now?" said Mason. "Only I'd really like to get out of here."

"We still need to collect the MSP backups," said Hunter.

"Oh, seriously? Weren't you planning to do that, like, a decade ago?" said Kearney.

"Well, I do beg your pardon," said Hunter, "but we got a bit distracted."

"So where are the backups?" said Mason before Kearney could

respond. "Not that I don't like a bit of hearty banter, but this really isn't the time or the place."

"That's why we're here, Trooper," said Captain Ryan. He was fumbling with his weapon, trying to fit a new magazine with shaking hands and failing dismally.

The members of Charlie Team watched for a few moments as the Marines checked the Mech corpses and secured the area. Then Hunter floated forward and took the magazine from Ryan.

"There's a knack, sir," he said, twisting the weapon around so that he could load the magazine. He gave it a smack, and it slotted into place.

"Thank you, er, Hunter," said Ryan. The captain gave a nervous laugh.

"First time in a firefight, sir?" asked Kearney, not unkindly.

"First time," said Ryan with a nod.

"Well, you've got the hang of it, sir," said Mason. "Shoot the enemy, don't die. That's really all there is to it."

"Makes sense," said Ryan, his voice shaking just a little. "Always knew you chaps had the easy part of the job."

"Don't worry," said Hunter, "the shaking's normal. Everyone does it, first time."

Sergeant Rodha gave a polite cough. "I don't like to interrupt, but we're not done yet."

Kearney nodded. "Right. MSP backups," she said, pulling herself back out into the corridor.

"Second door on the left," said Ryan. "Then it's an easy run to the waiting room outside the main bay, and a nice warm shuttle to the safety of *Vengeance*."

"Was that a mildly fatalistic joke, sir?" said Hunter.

"We'll make a Marine of you yet, sir," said Mason, slapping Ryan on the shoulder.

"Heaven forbid, Trooper," said Ryan fervently. "I don't think I could stand the excitement of doing this every day."

"Oh, you say that now, sir," said Mason, grinning inside his helmet, "but once it gets into your blood? Well, that's a different story."

"Yeah, but save it for another day," said Kearney. "Let's get the backups, then get the fuck out of here."

"Roger that," said Mason, "lead on, Macduff."

11

"Captain Ryan, how is the evacuation progressing?" said Stansfield on the command channel.

"We're removing the MSP backups at the moment; then we head for the shuttles," said Ryan.

"Good," said Stansfield, biting his tongue at Ryan's continued lack of respect. "What news from Lieutenant Fernandez? Is he with you?"

There was a pause before Ryan answered. "Nobody's seen Fernandez since he arrived on *Orion*."

"Then can I suggest you find him, Captain?" said Stansfield firmly. "I really don't want to lose my chief engineer."

"Of course, sir," said Ryan, "we'll do our best."

"Leave nobody behind," said Commander Vernon.

"That may be unavoidable," snapped Lieutenant Woodhall, inserting himself into the conversation like a knife between the ribs.

Vernon and Stansfield exchanged a glance across the bridge of *Vengeance*.

"We're at the main bay, and the crew have left or are boarding now," said Woodhall. "There's a shuttle for Captain Ryan and his team, but once that leaves, there'll be no way off *Orion*."

"Then I suggest *you* find Lieutenant Fernandez and his team and assist with their extraction," snapped Stansfield, "because there will be hell to pay if you leave them on *Orion* at the mercy of the Mechs. Is that clear, Lieutenant?"

"I don't think you quite understa–" Woodhall began.

"Don't tell me what I do and don't understand," thundered Stansfield, now properly angry. The bridge was silent as every eye turned to watch the admiral in full flow. "Find Fernandez and get his team safely off *Orion*, Lieutenant, or face a court-martial. Am I clear?"

"Sir," said Woodhall after a pause.

"Then get on with it. Stansfield out." He closed the channel and sat back in his chair. For a moment the bridge watched to see if anything more would happen. Then there was a cough, and the hum of professional chatter resumed as the crew returned to work.

"You think Woodhall will abandon Fernandez?" said Vernon.

Stansfield gave him a look, then shook his head. "Not if he knows what's good for him," growled the admiral.

"He has powerful friends," said Vernon. "Maybe he believes they'll protect him."

"Maybe they will," said Stansfield, "but we'll cross that bridge when we come to it. What news from the Battle Sphere?"

"Garbled, frankly," said Vernon, happy to change the subject. "Conway's got some plan to seize control of the Sphere, and Figgis is fighting a rear-guard action to hold the control room."

Stansfield shook his head. "Where did it all go wrong, eh, Ed? Nice easy mission, that's what they promised."

Vernon said nothing. The Admiralty's promises had never meant a great deal.

"Sir, you need to see this," said Lieutenant Yau, interrupting Stansfield's moment of quiet contemplation.

"Some good news, Lieutenant?" said Stansfield wearily. "You seem to be showing me more dull stars."

The main display was split to show views of the oncoming armada, the Battle Sphere, *Orion*, and the patch of space that contained the unlamented *Target One*. Except now, the circle of green that highlighted *Target One* was moving slowly across the field of stars.

"Oh, joy," said Vernon. "As if we didn't have enough problems."

"She's moving slowly, sir," said Yau, "but she's definitely moving."

"Her heading?" asked Stansfield.

"Uncertain, sir. She's certainly coming this way, but we can't tell if she's heading for us, for *Orion*, or for somewhere else entirely."

"The portal, maybe?" suggested Vernon.

"With our degraded sensors," said Yau apologetically, "it's impossible to say, sir, but that's certainly one possible explanation."

"How long till she gets here?" said Stansfield, cutting through the useless speculation.

Yau paused long enough that Stansfield tore his gaze from the main display to check that the lieutenant had heard the question. "Lieutenant?"

"Sorry, sir," said Yau. "I don't have a good answer for you, but it could be as much as two hours before *Target One* is within firing range."

"As long as that, eh?" said Stansfield. "Well, we'd better not waste any time." He flicked open the ship-wide channel. "*Vengeance*, this is Stansfield. The evacuation of *Orion* proceeds, but the threat is not yet over. An enemy battleship, designated *Target One*, will be within firing range in less than two hours. Prepare for action, and good luck to us all."

He switched to the command channel. "Ryan, Woodhall: be aware that *Target One* is beginning her next attack run. You have no more than ninety minutes to return to *Vengeance*."

"I thought you destroyed *Target One*, Admiral?" said Woodhall. "How is she still able to pose a threat?"

"Ninety minutes," said Ryan before Stansfield could reply, "understood. Woodhall, make sure the shuttles are loaded and ready to go as soon as both our team and Lieutenant Fernandez's reach the bay."

"But we don't know where Fernandez is," whined Woodhall, "he could be anywhere!"

"Then you'd better put some effort into finding him, Lieutenant," snapped Ryan.

"We're sending more shuttles to give you some options," said Vernon, "and we're also sending a couple to the Battle Sphere to bring back our people."

"Roger, thank you, Commander," said Ryan. "We have the MSP backups and are making our way to the main shuttle bay."

"Good to hear," said Stansfield, "but it's too soon to start smoking the kippers. Out."

"I'll update Conway," said Vernon, opening a channel. "This is Vernon. Are you able to talk?"

"Briefly, sir," said Conway, "we're about to get a bit busy."

"The enemy battleship, *Target One*, will be in firing range in less than two hours," said Vernon, speaking quickly, "just thought you should know."

There was a pause before Conway responded. "I think we'd better get on, sir," she said. "I'll update you as soon as I have news. Out."

"So where the hell is Fernandez?" said Ryan as he followed Kearney's team through a major hallway towards the main bay.

"I don't know, sir," snapped Kearney. They'd tried contacting the lieutenant, but either he wasn't receiving their messages, or he wasn't able to respond. Or both.

"I'll try him again," said Mason, opening a channel. "He's bound to, oh, is that you, Lieutenant Fernandez?"

"Of course it's bloody me," said Fernandez. "Who were you expecting, Gandhi?"

Mason nodded at the rest of the group and patched Fernandez into the team's channel. "You're in the public channel, sir. We thought we'd lost you."

"You might yet," said Fernandez. "We're not in the clear, and something's hunting us on this deck, something horrible."

"Is it a huge, fast-moving Mech?" said Hunter, thinking of the fate of Marine Petticrew.

"Could be," said Fernandez. "There's some weird stuff on this ship. We saw something, but there's no way of knowing if it was the thing that left the remains behind." He gave them a short summary of the loss of Tofler and Hurley. "There are things moving around up here. We can hear them."

"You have atmosphere?" said Mason. "Then we're coming to you. It's all a bit dark and cold down here."

"I don't think it's a good idea to come looking for us," said Midshipman York. "We'll meet near the main bay, if we can get there before the Mechs control the whole ship."

"We're coming to get you," said Captain Ryan. "Nobody gets left behind, not again."

"Thank you, sir, but the MSP backups should be the priority," said York. "We can't reach them from here, there's too much damage and we're too far away."

"We already have the backups, Midshipman," said Ryan, "so now we'll come to you."

"York's right, sir," said Fernandez. "Your priority is to get the backups away and preserve the mind states of the crew who've already died. We'll make our own way to the shuttles."

Ryan was silent for a moment. "I can't abandon you, Lieutenant," he said finally. "We need another solution."

"Think of it as rescuing the rest of the crew, sir, rather than abandoning us," said Fernandez.

"You're trying too hard to look on the bright side, Lieutenant," said Ryan, "but I can't fault your logic. I'll have Woodhall prep a shuttle for you."

"Roger that," said Fernandez. "See you back on *Vengeance*."

"How much further, York?" asked Fernandez as his small team floated through a large plant room. Fernandez wasn't sure of the purpose, but the equipment around them was almost entirely silent, powered down along with the reactors and now cold and dormant.

"Two more like this," said York, using the curved end of her crowbar to hook a grab handle and turn in mid-air. "Then we're back into the crew quarters and it should be a straight run."

"Heard that before," said Muller. He was running rear-guard, watching everything as they floated through the giant rooms. Here, amongst the machines, it was almost easy to forget that the ship was dead. The damage to this part of the ship was minimal, and if it weren't for the awful and unusual silence, he might have found the experience relaxing.

But the lack of light meant everything was shrouded in shadow, and shadow meant hiding places; fear of ambush meant this area was anything but relaxing. Deep pools of blackness were broken only by the light thrown by the team's helmet lamps and the occasional emergency warning or guidance lamp. Wherever the team turned, shapes loomed suddenly from the dark.

Debris and abandoned tools floated across the room, banging into walls or equipment. Every reflected flash of light or echoing clang triggered primal flight or fight responses and whipped the team's attention from their target.

"We're not evolved for this sort of challenge," said Fernandez, with one eye on the team's medical readouts. Even the Marines were stressed by the dark, their hearts racing as they floated through the huge space. "We need to get back to the smaller rooms where we've got a bit more control."

Douglas snorted but said nothing. Control was an illusion, especially in combat, and *Orion* was the very antithesis of a controlled environment.

"Crew quarters are smaller," said York, fighting hard to keep her panic at bay. She'd set her helmet lamps to flood the way ahead, but that just meant the shadows seemed deeper in her peripheral vision, where the unseen monsters lurked. The team had unconsciously closed up, keeping as close together as they could.

"Even the emergency lights aren't working down here," muttered York. "That's not a good sign, but there's the next door."

Ahead, a wall appeared at the edge of the lamplight, and the team hurried to reach it. The transient relief of reaching a verified land-mark faded quickly.

"No power," said York, "cranking manually." She released a panel in the wall and began turning the wheel that would open the door. It resisted, unused in years, but the suit's strength prevailed, and the wheel screeched as it began to turn and the doors edged slowly open. From the far end of the room there came an answering scream, as if something had heard the call of the door and was replying.

"What the hell was that?" said Fernandez, back against the wall and weapon facing into the darkness.

"Get the bloody door open," said Muller.

York nodded and went back to turning the wheel. Another scream reverberated through the thin air.

"It's coming closer," hissed Fernandez, swinging to point his weapon at the source of the scream.

"Or there's more than one of them?" said Muller.

"Got it," said York. She slipped through the open door into the room beyond. "Come on, come on," she hissed as she ripped the panel out of the wall to gain access to the wheel. The doors crept together until the gap was only half a metre wide.

"That'll do," said Fernandez, "we've got a shuttle to catch."

"And monsters to avoid," said York as the team began to work its way across the room.

Behind them, in the darkness, something screamed.

12

"Good thing we didn't come in through the front door," said Conway as she peered past Ten's shoulder into the central chamber.

"Right," said Ten, "but what do we do now?"

The room below held the core of the communications system that powered the Battle Sphere, as far as they could tell from the plans Davies had liberated. All they had to do was reach the floor, install the jumper to link Davies' console into the central network, and escape.

"This would be a lot easier without a squad of Mechs watching the inside of the door," said Ten. He shared the video from his HUD with Gray and Jackson. "Any ideas?"

"Throw a rock?" said Jackson. "Sorry, that's all I've got."

There was silence for a couple of moments, then Conway nodded. "Agreed, it's the only way." She looked around the team. "Who wants to be the rock?"

"Wait, what? What rock?" said Gray, confused.

"The rock," said Ten. "Paper, scissors, stone?"

"On three," said Conway, holding up her fist. "One, two, three – paper."

"Which loses to my scissors," said Ten, making a snipping motion with his fingers. "So I guess I'll be the stone."

"No, I'll do it," said Conway, but Ten shook his head.

"Better if I do it," he said, "but if you get out of this, make sure I get deployed back to a decent clone, will you?"

Conway stared at him, suddenly worried that this might be the last time she saw him, then nodded.

"Right," said Ten, making a move back down the corridor. "I'll work my way around and hit them from the other side. Don't be a stranger."

"Good luck," said Conway.

"And to you," replied Ten.

"I'll come with you," said Jackson suddenly. The others all looked at him. "A bigger rock will be more effective, and there's nothing I can do here to improve the odds." He nodded at Conway. "No room for three of us at that grill anyway."

"Thanks, Jackson," said Ten. Then he was off, Jackson following behind, leaving Conway and Gray alone in the small room at the end of a narrow passageway.

"So what now?" said Gray.

"Now," said Conway as she inspected her magazine and checked that her rifle's underslung grenade launcher was loaded, "we wait to see just how big a rock those two can sling."

"It's way too quiet," said Jackson as he and Ten hurried through the abandoned corridors of the Battle Sphere. "Where are all the Mechs?" They'd seen hardly any Mechs since leaving Davies in the command room, and everything felt spookily quiet.

"They'll be off bothering Figgis," said Ten, although he couldn't shake the feeling they were walking into a trap. "He'll be as happy as a pig in shit."

Jackson snorted. "You don't like him all that much, do you," he said. "What's going on between you two?"

Ten sighed. "I could tell you," he said, pausing at a junction to listen for Mechs, "but then I'd have to resuscitate you from boredom-inflicted heart failure."

He slipped around the corner and across the corridor, into what looked like a storage room. It was long and narrow, and the walls were lined with racks three metres high. The racks held large steel tanks, dozens of them.

"Is this oxygen?" asked Ten, tapping a long, pressurised cylinder.

"Could be," said Jackson. "And these look like they might be hydrogen, although why they'd be stockpiling gas is anyone's guess."

"Rocket fuel?" suggested Ten. "Or something for the discs?"

Jackson shrugged.

"Either way, it's a bit of luck for us," said Ten. "You thinking what I'm thinking?"

"An exploding rock?" said Jackson.

"I think we've taken that analogy as far as it can go," said Ten, "but basically, yes. Open the valves on a few of those cylinders while I just set up a couple of little mines."

Jackson walked down the room, opening valves as he went until gas hissed everywhere. Ten pulled a brick of plastic explosive from his pack and wedged it between a pair of cylinders. He added a detonator and linked it to his HUD, then stepped back to admire his work.

"Time to go," he said, satisfied. He hurried after Jackson, and the two Marines slid out into the corridor beyond.

"Should be about fifty metres that way," said Jackson as they crept along a walkway that took them between two blocks. Below, a cavernous room stretched a hundred metres in either direction.

"The Mechs' storage bay?" said Ten.

They passed through the door on the far side of the walkway and ghosted along another corridor.

"This is it," said Ten as they reached the end. "Ready?" he asked, checking his rifle. Jackson nodded. "Conway, get ready to move."

"Roger that," said Conway.

"Time for a little disruption," said Ten, triggering the detonator.

There was a distant bang, followed by a huge roar. The floor shook, and a great cloud of smoke rolled out into the corridor.

"On three," said Jackson, his own weapon raised.

"Three," said Ten, and the two Marines charged around the corner, firing as they went.

The hall outside the central chamber was wide and open, and a squad of Mechs stood guard. Several had already moved to investigate the explosion, and the others were caught by surprise. As Ten and Jackson charged into the open, the Mechs fell back, firing indiscriminately as they went, spraying the area with bullets.

Jackson spun away, struck in the chest, and his rifle clattered across the floor.

Ten targeted the closest Mech, firing repeatedly. The machine fell back, helmet blasted to pieces, and Ten dived into cover behind a broad girder that soared towards the roof.

"Jackson, get up!" he yelled. "Move!" but the man just lay there: stunned or dead, Ten couldn't tell. He leaned out and fired again into the squad of Mechs, killing another, then ducked back as the girder pinged under heavy fire.

"Jackson, stay down!" yelled Ten. "Grenades," he said, tossing a pair of grenades towards the Mechs. Without waiting for the detonations, he spun around the girder again and triggered the rifle's grenade launcher, sending a round towards the doors of the central chamber. As the grenades detonated, he fired again at the Mechs, holding his finger on the trigger to spray rounds across the hall. From inside the central chamber, he could hear more firing as Conway and Gray made their presence known.

Ten grinned and stepped back into cover behind the girder, reloading his rifle as he went. But before he could do more, the shooting stopped and silence fell. He paused for a count of three, then peeked out.

The doors to the central chamber had buckled and twisted, but they were still locked closed. In front of them, a dozen Mechs were sprawled in various stages of dismemberment. None moved.

"Jackson," hissed Ten, "you can get up now!"

"Shit," said Jackson as he levered himself to his feet and shook his head, "everything hurts."

Ten nodded and padded across the hall, rifle raised. He walked cautiously up to the nearest Mech, rammed a booted foot into its throat, and shot the OctoBot before it could detach from its carrier's skull. He then worked methodically around the hall as Jackson retrieved his rifle, shooting each of the Mechs in turn to make sure they were truly dead. By the time he reached the doors of the central chamber, Jackson was back in action and watching for new enemies.

"Conway, you done yet?" said Ten, shooting the last of the Mechs.

"Working on it," said Conway. "This isn't as easy as it looks."

"Well, don't take too long," said Ten.

"We'll never get these doors open," said Jackson as he sidled up to them, glancing at the scorched metal as he scanned the hall for new enemies. "We aren't going home that way."

"Agreed," said Ten, "so we'll just stay out here and keep an eye on things."

"You do that," snapped Conway, "and shut up while I get this done."

Ten and Jackson dragged a handful of Mech corpses into a crude pile and crouched behind them outside the ruined doors, peering out at the world and expecting attack at any moment.

"Done," said Conway suddenly, and Ten almost jumped out of his skin. "Davies is doing his shit, and we need to get out of here."

"Roger that," said Ten, relieved. "You ready to move, then?"

"Just setting out a few presents for our chums to make sure they can't come back here and do anything we don't like," said Conway.

"Explosive presents, by any chance?" said Ten. "My favourite type."

"This is Davies," said Davies in the team channel. "I've got access again. I'll be back in control in a few minutes, but the Sphere is wrecked and we've got only minimal systems."

"So you won't be flying us home, eh, Double-D?" said Ten.

"Not a chance, mate," said Davies. "Shuttles, yeah?"

"Shuttles," agreed Ten. "Time to go, Conway?"

"Shuttles," said Conway, "and back to *Vengeance* in time for kippers."

Jackson stood up from his crouch, marks standing out on his armour where the Mechs' attacks had knocked him over. He took a few steps across the hallway, following the route to the main bay highlighted in his HUD, then stopped, rifle raised. "There's something moving out here, Ten," he said, taking a careful step to his left. "You hear that?"

"I heard it," said Ten. He reloaded his grenade launcher as he moved out of Jackson's shadow to cover his flank. "You'd better go, Conway," he said. "Looks like we might be a while."

13

"Is it still behind us?" said Muller as he floated backwards, rifle trained back the way they had come and helmet lamps flooding a few metres of grimy equipment. They were halfway across the third of the huge equipment rooms that York's route was taking them through, and it was no less dark and unpleasant than the first two.

"Maybe we got it," said Douglas as she scanned the way ahead. "Maybe there was only one, and we killed it back in the lift."

"That would be nice," muttered York, but they all knew it wasn't true. Even without the noises, none of them would have believed that there was nothing following them – stalking them – through the bowels of the abandoned ship.

And they were still hearing noises. York had half-convinced herself that they were just the normal mechanical sounds of a working starship. But then something had screeched – a sound like the cry of a hunting eagle – and she'd hurried on, desperate to avoid meeting the owner of that hideous call.

After that, the noises kept coming. Infrequent and distant, at first, but now they were getting closer and more frequent. Sometimes it seemed that they were coming from more than one direction. At other times, they'd hear several cries echoing through the ship, as if a pack had howled in the dark. The team pushed through the cavernous rooms as quickly as they could, closing and locking doors behind them.

They paused at a crossroads, an open area between the huge machines where the engineers and technicians had built an informal coffee station. The coffee machine was still there, but the liquid was gone, splashed across the floor and frozen solid before the artificial gravity had failed.

"I know where we are," said York, her foot hooked around a grab rail. "Used to come here to snatch a drink between shifts. We're close. Another hundred metres that way, then we're back into the crew quarters and the smaller corridors and rooms."

"That way?" said Douglas, pointing her shotgun in the direction York had indicated. The lamp beneath the barrel of the assault weapon played its light across huge racks of equipment before being swallowed by the darkness.

"Yeah," said York. "You ready to–"

A scream cut through the thin air, closer and louder than any they'd heard before.

"That came from over there," said Muller, twisting to peer into the gloom, his lamps layering shadows on top of Douglas'. "Volunteers?" he muttered.

Then a second cry floated through the enormous room.

"They're ahead of us," said York. "How's that possible?"

"They're smart," said Fernandez, "and they're guided by something with a rudimentary sense of tactics."

Another scream echoed through the hall, and the team spun around, looking back the way they'd come.

"Surrounded," said Muller, panning his lamps across the hall, searching for the enemy.

"Only a 'rudimentary sense', sir?" said York.

"We need another way out of here," said Fernandez, ignoring her question. "What's that way?" he said, pointing between the equipment at right angles to their direction of travel.

"The hull," said York. "We'll have to go the other way and double around. It's longer, but we'll be back in the personnel corridors."

"Easier to see what's coming," said Douglas.

"But harder to avoid it when it does," said Muller.

More screams sounded in the dark, and Fernandez shook his head, mind made up. "Go that way," he said.

"My turn on point?" said Muller, pushing forward into the gloom.

Douglas grabbed York's arm before she could leave. "Take this," she said, offering a pistol handle first. "More effective than a club," she said, nodding at York's crowbar.

"Thanks," said York, taking the pistol and checking the magazine. "Didn't think I'd ever need to be armed on my own bloody ship."

"Are we moving?" snapped Fernandez. Douglas nodded, and York pushed away from the railing, pulling herself along in Muller's wake. Fernandez followed quickly, leaving Douglas alone with the coffee machine. She paused, oriented herself on the railing, then flicked off her lamps and swam silently through the darkness, gaze locked on the lights ahead.

"You get the feeling we're being herded?" said Douglas. The team had found an exit from the equipment room, and now they were in a service corridor, working their way around the edge of the cavernous space. The emergency lighting cast a dull red glow over the corridor, making everything look grimly unpleasant.

"No sign of the Mechs," said Muller, who was still leading the way. "Maybe we've lost them."

Fernandez shook his head. "Keep your eyes open," he said.

As if to validate his warning, a cry sounded from ahead.

"That's bloody close," said Muller, pulling himself to a halt against a pipe.

The service corridor was barely wide enough for the armoured Marines, but it had plenty of cubby holes and junctions.

"Good place for an ambush," said Douglas as the team eased forward, bunched up behind Muller.

"Keep going," said Fernandez. "We can't stay here forever."

Muller nodded and kicked away from the pipe to float a little further down the corridor, rifle up and ready.

"Contact!" yelled Douglas, and suddenly her shotgun was booming. Something screamed as the team turned; then York's pistol popped, the noise all but lost under the shattering roar of the shotgun.

Fernandez could only watch, staring past Douglas, as a huge Mech pulled itself along the corridor, arms outstretched and mouth open as it screamed at its prey.

"Another," said Muller, barely getting the word out before he began firing at a second Mech that appeared at the edge of his torchlight. It moved with ferocious speed, talon-tipped fingers reaching for him as the thing screamed hideously.

Muller focused and squeezed the trigger, drilling the Mech with two three-round bursts. The first tore through the creature's open mouth and destroyed its spine; the second mostly ricocheted harmlessly away, turned aside by the Mech's heavily-armoured shoulders.

Muller palmed the body aside, twisting around so that the Mech slammed into the ceiling, then cart-wheeled into the team. Muller heaved himself clear, checked the corridor was clear, then turned to look the other way.

"Move," he yelled, trying to get a clear shot at the other Mech as it roared along the corridor towards Douglas. But Fernandez either didn't hear, or he didn't understand. He hung in the narrow space like an ugly bauble, a useless decoration.

The second Mech screamed as Douglas shot it in the head, heavy skull turning aside the worst of the blast. Still the thing came on, smashing into Douglas and clawing at her even as she blasted it to pieces. The force of the collision carried her back into York and then Fernandez, pushing them all back along the corridor.

Douglas yelled; then everything fell silent. Muller pushed his way past York and Fernandez and shoved at the dead Mech, forcing it away from Douglas. Then he put a bracing foot against a wall, set the barrel of his rifle against the Mech's head, and put three rounds through its skull.

"And stay down," he said as he pushed the corpse away. He turned back to the others, who were staring at him. "Watch out for more of them," he snapped, pointing along the corridor.

The two officers nodded and turned, pistols pointing uncertainly along the passage as they stared through a cloud of Mech blood and snatched worried glances at the two Marines.

"Douglas," said Muller as he tapped into her medical readouts, "talk to me. You okay?"

"Hip's fucked," hissed Douglas through gritted teeth, "suit integrity compromised."

Muller glanced down at Douglas' waist and swore. Bright marks showed along the armour, and blood was seeping out of a gash in the suit above her left hip. The medical information wasn't encouraging.

"Leave me," said Douglas. "You've got my backup, right?" The Marines were cross-protected, their mind states backing up to each other's suits before handing off to the closest independent MSP system.

"Shut up," snapped Muller as he pulled a kit from a pocket on his chest. He sprayed something into the gashed armour, and Douglas gasped as the open wounds were filled with foam that quickly set hard.

There was a scream from along the corridor. Another Mech, still hunting in the darkness. Fernandez and York tensed, staring along the passage.

"Opioids for you, I think," said Muller, ignoring the activity around him and triggering the dispensary in Douglas' suit.

"Ah," said Douglas dreamily as the drugs took hold. "That's the only good bit about getting shot." She looked at Muller as he checked her armour for more damage. "You leaving me here, Muller?"

"Yeah," said Muller distractedly as he retrieved his rifle. "You're a pain in the neck, Douglas."

He grabbed her shotgun, released the tether from York's suit, and reloaded it. "Ma'am, take this," he said, passing the shotgun to York. "You know how to use it?"

"Not really," said York, sounding distinctly unexcited at the prospect.

"Point that end at the bad guys," said Muller, gently pushing the tip of the barrel away so that it pointed along the corridor, "squeeze the trigger, pray. And link it to your HUD so that you have ammo readouts and reload prompts, okay?"

Another scream, much closer than before, and they all turned to face the noise.

"Sir," said Muller, tugging gently on Fernandez's arm and horribly aware that he was, as the only combat-experienced person still operational, now the de facto commander of the mission, "hold on to Douglas, sir. Make sure she's still with us when we move, right? Don't leave her behind."

"Wait, what?" said Fernandez, but Muller had already moved away.

"We're going," said Muller, taking point and kicking the corpse of the Mech he'd killed out of the way. "Don't shoot me with that thing, ma'am," he said, nudging the shotgun so that York wasn't aiming at him.

"Of course," said York with a small cough. "Sorry."

"And aim for the head," said Muller, "that's their vulnerable spot."

York nodded. "That's everybody's vulnerable spot," she muttered as Muller pushed off along the corridor, his rifle leading the way.

"Fernandez, this is Woodhall," said a new voice in the team's channel. "Where are you?"

"Er, deck six," said Fernandez, checking his HUD, "heading to the crew quarters, but–"

"Hurry it up," interrupted Woodhall. "The shuttle can't wait any longer. You've got five minutes. Out."

"Hold on," said Fernandez, but Woodhall had already left the channel. Fernandez tried to open another, but Woodhall's HUD was set to refuse his requests.

"What the hell?" muttered Fernandez with a frown. He set a timer in his HUD, then opened a channel to Kearney and her team. "What's going on? Woodhall's just given me a five-minute departure warning, and we're not going to get there in time. I thought we had a shuttle?"

"No idea," said Kearney, "but Ryan's spitting teeth. We're hustling, but it sounds like that little shit is gearing up to dump us here."

"Roger," said Fernandez, snagging Douglas' shoulder to keep her moving in the right direction. "Good luck." He switched back to the team channel. "We've got five minutes. How far is it now?" he asked.

"We're close," said York as they crossed a junction and moved into a more spacious crew area. She kept glancing back at Douglas, who floated along behind Fernandez, dragged along in a drug-fuelled daze. "It's that way," she said, pointing at a door at the end of a short corridor, "then across the mess, out the other side, up two decks, and we're there."

Muller checked the side corridors, then pushed over to the door and peered through the inspection glass. "Vacuum," he said, tapping a warning indicator in the door. "Is this the only way?"

"There're other ways," said York unenthusiastically, "but we'll never get there in time. This is–" A scream sounded from behind them, far too close for comfort and quickly followed by a second, then a third. York coughed nervously as the screams sounded again, closer. "This is the fastest route."

She signalled for Muller to open the door, but Fernandez put a hand on the Marine's arm.

"Hold on a moment," said Fernandez. "I think we can kill two birds with one stone. York, will this door open even though there's a vacuum on the far side?"

"Yes," she said, accessing the door's control system through her HUD. "It has power, I can override the safety protocols."

"Then here's what we do," said Fernandez, outlining his plan. He looked around at the team, but nobody had anything to add except Douglas, who burbled happily about nothing at all. "Move," he said, shooing at the others.

The team moved, taking up their stations only just in time. Fernandez hung in front of the door, one hand firmly gripping a tether. At the far end of the corridor, he watched as a Mech came into sight.

"Here we go," he muttered as the thing screamed at him. Two more followed, and then all three were charging down the corridor, heaving themselves along in a frenzy.

Fernandez watched them coming, judging the moment. The things were ferociously fast.

"Pull," he yelled. Mason heaved on the tether, and Fernandez floated away from the door into the side corridor. The Mechs screamed again, sensing that the chase was on.

Fernandez grabbed a handrail and locked his suit glove closed. "Now, York."

York triggered the door controls. Nothing happened. The Mechs screamed, and York gibbered inside her helmet as she searched out the problem.

"York!" shouted Mason. "Open the fucking door!"

And suddenly the door slid back. A breeze began to flow as the door opened; then it picked up as the atmosphere vented into the vacuum beyond the door. In seconds it went from a gentle breeze to a howling vortex. The three huge Mechs were caught in the winds, swept along ever faster as the atmosphere whipped out of the holes in *Orion*'s hull.

The first of the Mechs flailed along the corridor, talons leaving bright marks on the walls as the creature tried desperately to slow its headlong plunge. Then it flashed across the open space and smashed into the doorframe. Blood exploded into the air and was whipped away as the Mech howled its anger. Then it was gone, dragged out into the room beyond.

The second Mech threw out its arms and snatched at the doorframe, holding itself in the middle of the storm, refusing to give in. Then the third Mech barrelled into it and both were swept through the doorway, across the room and out through the great hole in *Orion*'s hull.

Moments later, the wind died to nothing as the last of the atmosphere in that part of the ship escaped into the void. The team hung in space for a moment; then Fernandez coughed and released his grip on the rail.

"That was exciting," he muttered, flexing his fingers to work some life back into his hand.

Then the shuttle departure counter reached zero and pinged gently in his HUD. "Oh, shit."

14

"Move!" shouted Hunter, waving the team through the doorway and counting them as they went. He hung to one side, back against the wall, as the first Mechs appeared on the far side of the room. "Just fucking die already," he snapped as he fired on the lead Mech. It collapsed, chest a ruined mess, and its corpse bounced gently off the wall as the other Mechs darted for cover.

Kearney took station on the other side of the door and fired on the Mechs, holding them off. "I'm out," she said suddenly, ejecting the empty magazine from her rifle.

"Last one," said Marine Hamilton, passing over a magazine as he followed the rest of the team. Kearney took it with a nod and reloaded her rifle. She pushed herself away from the wall and fired off two bursts at the Mechs, using the recoil to push her gently backwards through the doorway.

"One more room," said Ryan. He paused inside the doorway and fired his captured weapon at the Mechs twenty metres away.

Hunter shook his head as the last of the Marines ducked out into the next room. He let go one last burst at the advancing Mechs, then pulled himself around the doorframe as a flurry of enemy fire chewed at the walls.

Ryan slapped the door control, and it slid closed. Then he used his executive authority to lock the door.

"That ought to hold them," he said smugly, although nothing else had really slowed the Mechs in their pursuit.

When Hunter looked for the rest of the team, they were already crossing the room, heading for the airlock that would lead them to the transport shuttles.

"Where's Woodhall?" snarled Ryan, looking around the room. "I'd expected him to be here."

"And what about Lieutenant Fernandez?" said Kearney. "

"In the airlock, maybe?" said Hunter as the two men pushed off their wall and floated across the waiting room.

"He's not here," said Mason from the head of the small column. "The airlock is open at both ends, and there's nobody here but us chickens."

"Just tell me there are shuttles waiting to take us to *Vengeance*," said Hunter as he reached the airlock's inner door.

"You're not going to believe this," said Mason, the tone of his voice firmly indicating his own disbelief, "but there actually *is* a ship waiting for us. Several, in fact, although they're all pretty beaten up." He cleared his throat. "All aboard, ladies and gentlemen. This will be the last flight from HMS *Orion*, and you really don't want to get left behind."

"That thing?" said Kearney incredulously as she reached Mason's station in the airlock and peered out into the bay. With most of the lights extinguished, it was impossible to gauge the true scale of the bay, but the range finders in her HUD indicated that the inside of the hull was more than a hundred metres from the airlock. "It looks dead."

Mason could only agree. "She does look a little the worse for wear," he said, "but it's either the one that's past her best," he said, nodding at the shuttle, "or one of the flying coffins over there."

Kearney looked at the only other ships in the bay and snorted. "Are those *Vengeance*'s fighter-bombers? They're fucking antiques!"

"Right," agreed Mason, "so we'll take the shuttle, right? What choice do we have?"

"None whatsoever," said Kearney.

"Can we get going?" said Sergeant Rodha. "Only it's getting a bit cramped in here." The airlock was crowded with armoured Marines, and more waited outside.

Kearney glanced sceptically at the shuttle again, then nodded. "Go," she said to Rodha, waving him out of the airlock.

The sergeant, ever cautious, checked the huge bay for signs of movement or activity, then slid out of the airlock, staying close to the outer doors. He activated the magnetic clamps on his boots, stood on the wall above the airlock, and used the scope of his rifle to scan the bay.

The shuttle was at the end of a pier, twenty metres from the airlock, clamped to a landing pad. "Ogilvie, Egan. Get a line out to that shuttle," said Rodha. "Try not to damage it any further. Hamilton, cover them. Get moving, people."

Marine Ogilvie floated out of the airlock and clamped her boots to the wall. Egan came next, tethering to Ogilvie before pushing off the wall to float towards the shuttle. He landed feet first on the hull of the shuttle and clamped down. "One small step for man," he said solemnly. "Might be better to float back to *Vengeance*, Sarge. This thing's ready for the scrapyard."

"Stop fucking around," snapped Rodha.

"I'm on it," said Egan cheerfully. He unclipped the cable and made his way to the shuttle's airlock. "Should this be open?" he said as he tied the cable to an attachment point next to the airlock. He waved at Ogilvie. "All done."

She nodded back and tied off her end of the cable, then looked up to signal to Egan.

"Behind you," she shouted, unslinging her weapon. Egan stared at her for a second, then spun around, fumbling for his rifle.

An armoured Mech emerged from the depths of the shuttle and flew at Egan. It smashed into him, knocking him out of the airlock into *Orion*'s bay, his rifle floating uselessly away.

"Help!" yelped Egan as he grappled with the huge Mech. Egan was half-crushed as his back slammed into the pier and the Mech's mass pressed down on him, then their momentum carried them away, a tumbling mess of limbs.

The other Marines scrambled out into the bay, boots clamped to the walls and walkways, as Ogilvie pointed and yelled. The Marines spread out, confused and all looking for a clear shot at the Mech.

"Just fucking shoot it!" yelled Egan as the Mech pulled at his arm, one knee braced on the Marine's chest for leverage. Egan punched at the Mech's head and arms with his free hand, striking out at anything he could reach, but unable to land a telling blow. Mech and Marine tumbled faster, spinning more quickly as they drifted across the bay, getting further and further from the airlock.

"Argh!" Egan's scream was raw as the Mech heaved on his arm, both hands wrapped around the Marine's wrist. Then Egan screamed again, and suddenly he was free of the Mech as the creature lost its position and flipped backwards.

A metre of clear space opened between them and Rodha opened fire, his rifle flaring silently in the vacuum. Ogilvie fired as well, and then all the Marines were firing, blazing away at the Mech as it tumbled across the bay.

"I think it's dead," said Kearney as the Mech twitched and jerked. The firing stopped as quickly as it had started, and the Mech's shattered corpse floated away, turning slowly as it went.

"Oh, shit, Egan," said Rodha, and attention flipped back to the stricken Marine. He tumbled slowly, trailing a fine cloud of freezing blood as he went. Ogilvie yelled, and Kearney grabbed her arm.

"Let me go!" she snapped, twisting to free herself.

But Kearney held her and shook her head. "He's dead, Ogilvie," she said firmly. "Check the readouts."

Ogilvie paused; then she swore and yanked her arm free. "Fuck it," she said, "that's no way to go."

"His mind state's safe," said Rodha. "There's nothing more we can do for him except escape, so focus on that. Right, Ogilvie?"

Ogilvie was silent for a few moments, staring out across the bay; then she nodded. "Sarge," she said, coldly professional.

"Right," said Rodha, "so let's get over there and check for more of the bastard things."

Ogilvie nodded and reloaded her rifle, then pulled herself along the line to the shuttle. Hamilton followed, and the two Marines disappeared into the small ship as the others started to cross the bay.

"Clear," said Ogilvie a few moments later. "But we need a pilot."

"Just get aboard," growled Rodha, "and we'll sort it out later."

The Marines began to flow across the bay, following Ogilvie's tethered line. Sergeant Rodha counted them out and watched each embark in turn.

Captain Ryan was one of the last to go. He stood near the airlock, boots clamped to the wall, staring at the damage done to his ship by the Mechs. "Doesn't look so bad from in here," he said, although he had to admit that the gaping hole did little for *Orion's* battle readiness.

"You able to pilot a shuttle, sir?" said Rodha, interrupting Ryan's inspection.

"Yes, Sergeant," said the captain, "strictly speaking. But it's been years."

"Well, now would be a great time to refresh your memory, sir," said Rodha in the calm voice used by NCOs to nudge reluctant officers onto the true and obvious path. "Just so we're not all stuck here till the Mechs finish slicing up *Orion*, sir."

"I'm not sure that's a good idea, Sergeant," said Ryan. "Captains don't tend to fly much, as a rule."

"None of my team is qualified to pilot anything larger than a golf cart, sir," said Rodha, "and this isn't the best time to learn, so maybe you could prep the shuttle and hope it comes back to you? Before we all die, sir."

Ryan gave a last look around the bay, then nodded. "Yes, well," he said. "When you put it like that. I'll see what I can do." The captain hauled himself across the bay towards the shuttle, and Rodha shook his head in wonder at the working of the officer class.

"We're done here," he said to Kearney as the last Marine boarded the shuttle. "You ready to go?"

Charlie Team were clustered at the airlock.

"Fernandez isn't here yet," said Kearney.

"Right, yeah. So we wait," said Rodha. "No problem with that."

The channel was silent for a moment; then Kearney shook her head. "Negative, Sergeant," she said. "You go, we'll wait for Fernandez and his team."

"On your own?" said Rodha. "I don't think so. We'll unload half the team and prepare a defensive position, then settle in to wait."

"No," said Kearney sharply. "You've got the MSP backups and Ryan. Get to *Vengeance*, make sure everyone's safe. We'll be on the second shuttle before you've finished docking."

"I don't like it," said Rodha.

"But you know it's the right thing to do," said Mason. "Fernandez'll be here in a few minutes, and we'll be on that shuttle faster than a pack of greased whippets."

Rodha was silent for several seconds while he thought it over. "Find out where Fernandez is," he said eventually. "I want to know you're not embarking on some fool's errand before I leave you here."

"Deal," said Kearney, opening a channel. "Lieutenant Fernandez, are you there?"

"Kearney?" came the reply. "Are you still on *Orion*?"

"Yes, sir," said Kearney, "we're in the bay with the shuttle, waiting to leave. You coming?"

"We're in a bit of trouble," said Fernandez. "We're pinned down by Mechs. There's no way we'll be able to reach the bay."

"How many Mechs?" asked Mason.

"Er, all of them, I think," said Fernandez. "There's no way out of here. Get on the shuttle and go."

"Where are you, sir?" said Kearney.

"This is York," said a second voice. "We're one deck up and twenty metres forward of your position in a stairwell."

Kearney flicked through the plans for *Orion* until she found the location. "I've got you, ma'am," she said, "we're coming to you. Stay in this channel."

"You sure you don't want us to come with you?" Rodha said to Kearney in a private channel.

"No," said Kearney, "you've done enough. Get back to *Vengeance* and see to your people."

"Roger," said Rodha, clearly not keen to stay on the doomed battleship any longer than necessary. For a moment it looked like he might say something profound; then he nodded. "We'll have the kippers waiting for you." He turned towards the shuttle and waved, and Ogilvie pushed something along the tether.

"A parting gift," said Rodha as the bag floated serenely across the bay. He unclipped it and passed it to Mason. "That's all the ammo we have left. Make it count."

"Thanks, Sarge," said Kearney, passing magazines from the bag to Mason and Hunter. "Now get going. We'll be right behind you."

Rodha nodded, grabbed hold of the tether and hauled himself across the bay to the shuttle. He paused at the airlock to unclip the tether and wave to Charlie Team; then he disappeared into the shuttle and the hatch closed behind him.

"I guess we're on our own again," said Mason, checking his rifle.

"I guess we are," said Kearney. "Let's go find some officers."

"Great," said Hunter. "As if we weren't in enough trouble."

15

"They're on their way," said York to Muller, "but I've no idea how they'll get here."

"Great," said Muller absentmindedly. He was pounding a Mech's head with his booted foot, stamping it into the wall to make sure the OctoBot couldn't detach itself, a task that was dramatically more difficult without gravity to hold him in place. He paused, inspected the damage, then liberated the creature's weapon and checked the magazine before kicking the corpse away.

"Do you enjoy your work?" asked Fernandez as he watched Muller settle back against the wall, sighting down the barrel of his stolen weapon as he waited for the next wave of enemies. "The risk and the violence, I mean."

"It has its moments," said Muller. He fired a few rounds at a brace of Mechs who edged cautiously around the corner. They ducked quickly out of sight, and Muller shifted position to wait for them to reappear. "But it's been a long day, and I'm bloody knackered."

The two Mechs popped back up, floating aggressively from cover and firing at Muller's old position as they came. Muller calmly shot them, drilling each Mech with a neat burst of fire and then, when he was sure they were dead, shooting them again to kill the OctoBots.

"I mean, today is a bit special," said Muller as he moved position to fire a short burst into the stairwell. "Most days aren't like this."

"Really?" said York, fascinated despite herself.

"Yeah. I mean, we do lots of training and practice, and we spend a lot of time on the range," said Muller, "but we get precious little real action. Not like this." He paused to cross the stairwell and fire at a Mech coming from the other direction. It reeled away, trailing fluid, as Muller reached the wall and checked his magazine. "But this sort of makes it all worthwhile."

"I'm glad you're having so much fun," said York drily.

"It's fun, but I'm ready to call it a day, to be honest," said Muller with a glance at Douglas, who was drugged up to the eyeballs and floating behind Lieutenant Fernandez. "I think we're due some downtime."

"Roger that," said York with feeling.

"And I've no idea how we get out of this," said Muller. He eased forward to peer over the stairwell railing, but ducked quickly back as gunfire erupted from the next deck. "These bastards are persistent, and there's a hell of a lot of them. It's only a matter of time..." He trailed off, unwilling to finish the sentence.

"Before they storm our position and kill us all?" said York.

"Yeah," muttered Muller. "Sorry to be so down on the situation, but I think we're probably fucked." He fired at a shadow on the stairwell as Fernandez fired the other way from the far end of the landing.

"Muller, this is Kearney," said a new voice in the channel. "Where exactly are you?"

"Stairwell fourteen, on the landing between decks, er, six and seven," said Muller, glancing at the numbers stencilled on the walls. "You coming down from seven or up from six?"

"Neither," said Kearney. "Stay on the landing. Mason's going to do something dramatic."

"Dramatic?" said Fernandez.

"She means 'loud', I think, sir," translated Muller.

Fernandez frowned. "But we're in a vacuum," he said in a confused tone. "How can anything be loud?"

"Figuratively speaking, sir," said Muller, "but – *shit!*"

There was a flurry of motion from decks six and seven as the Mechs made a concerted effort to end the stand-off. A squad appeared in front of Muller and York, firing as they came.

York was yelling as she fired, her finger pressed hard down on the shotgun's trigger as bullets ricocheted from walls, ceiling and armour. Muller sprayed fire into the Mechs as they pushed into the stairwell from deck six and tried to close the distance with the Marines.

"Fuck!" yelped Fernandez as he fired at the Mechs coming from deck seven, but his puny pistol hardly slowed them.

"Kearney!" shouted Muller. "Now!"

"Patience, Muller," said Kearney. "These things take time to do right."

"We're fucking out of time!" yelled Muller as he exhausted his magazine and the gun stopped firing. "Shit!" He threw the gun at the nearest Mech and pulled out a pistol. The incoming fire pinged against his suit until all he could hear were the dings and cracks of bullets on armour.

Then the firing stopped, and Muller looked up to see a Mech bearing down on him. "Shit," he said again as the Mech closed to grappling distance and knocked away his flailing pistol, sending it spinning across the stairs.

Muller punched at the Mech, desperate to land a telling blow as the creature tried to unscrew his helmet. Another Mech grabbed his legs; then a third wrapped its arms around his waist.

"Get off me," said Muller, striking out and trying to push the Mechs away, punching and clawing at them all in a sudden panic.

There was a blinding flash of light, and for a moment the Mechs froze, silhouetted against the glare. Then the dull red gloom of the emergency lights returned, and Charlie Team appeared through a new hole in the wall, firing as they came. The Mechs fell back, shocked by the sudden appearance of new enemies and blasted apart by Charlie Team's controlled fire. In moment it was over, and the Mechs were dead, or scattered and retreating.

Muller shook himself loose from the Mech that had grabbed his waist, levering its dead arms away so that he could push it away. "And stay down," he muttered as the creature floated loose.

Not that there was much space left in the stairwell. Mech corpses, spent bullets and shell casings, body parts and frozen bio-mechanical fluids filled the small space, and Charlie Team had to haul things around and wade through the mess to uncover Lieutenant Fernandez and his team.

"Good to see you, sir," said Mason as Kearney and Hunter covered the stairs to decks six and seven. "But let's get moving, shall we? They won't stay cowed for long."

Fernandez nodded quickly, stunned into silence by the sudden appearance of Charlie Team and the abrupt change in their fortunes.

"Douglas is injured," said Muller as he grabbed his floating pistol and checked the magazine. "Hole in her leg."

"Mmm, but the drugs," said Douglas dozily.

"And out of it," Muller added, grabbing Douglas's arm and towing her toward the new hole in the wall.

"Anything else we need to know?" said Kearney as Mason led Fernandez away.

"Tofler and Hurley are dead," said York as she followed Fernandez. "But we secured the reactors, so there's no chance of *Orion* blowing herself to smithereens."

"Move!" said Hunter, appearing at the rear of the group. "They're coming, and there's a hell of a lot of them."

Mason swore and pulled himself along the corridor as fast as he could go. The others followed as Kearney and Hunter took turns to work a zero-G version of the bounding overwatch technique the Marines normally used to advance under fire.

"Too slow," said Kearney as Mason's party turned a corner and disappeared from sight. She hauled herself after Hunter; then together they turned at the end of the corridor and waited for the Mechs. "Are you sure they were coming this way?" said Kearney after a few seconds.

"They were definitely moving," said Hunter. "Thought they were right behind us."

Kearney paused for a few seconds, then shook her head. "Go," she said, pushing away from the wall, "go!"

"Yeah," said Hunter, grabbing a handle to pull himself along the corridor, "something's not right."

The two troopers moved as fast as they could, heading back to the airlock. They turned the last corner to see Mason ahead of them, waiting at the airlock's inner door, waving them on.

"Come on," said Mason, "the others are boarding, we need to get out of here."

"Roger that," said Kearney as she reached the airlock. "Was worried something had gone wrong," she said as they all moved through the open airlock.

"Nah," said Mason as he floated out of the outer door into the main shuttle bay, "everything's good. Our vessel awaits." He waved towards one of the beaten-up old fighters. "She looks like shit, but that's our ticket out of here."

Then he turned quickly when Kearney swore.

Through a hole in the wall, a hundred metres from the airlock, Mechs were launching themselves into the bay.

"The sneaky fuckers," said Hunter. "I knew they were up to something."

"You know how to fly this thing, right?" said Muller as he squeezed his armoured bulk into the cramped quarters behind the fighter-bomber's tiny flight deck.

"This 'thing'?" said York. "Her name is *Stockton*. There was probably a reason for that when she was launched. And yes, I know how to fly her. Standard controls, even though she's at least as ancient as *Vengeance*."

"We're loaded," said Fernandez from the rear of the ship, "airlock is closed, just waiting for Charlie Team."

"Time to go home," muttered York. "Pressurising now," she said, punching a button on *Stockton*'s control panel. "Here comes the air."

She paused, then unclipped and removed her helmet. It clipped neatly into place on a magnetic latch behind the pilot's chair as she slipped behind the controls.

"Lights, cameras," she muttered, flicking at the control panel. The screens came on as the little ship came alive, and York ran a practiced eye over the readouts. "And action. Reactor's working at full capacity, weapons are charged and armed, engines are ready. Everything seems to be in order," she said calmly as she completed her pre-flight check.

"What's keeping them?" said Fernandez.

"Charlie Team, sir?" said York with a frown. "They were right behind us." She flicked at the panel and opened a channel. "Mason, are you joining us?"

"Just waiting for Hunter and Kearney, ma'am," said Mason, "then we'll be right there. And here they are now."

York whistled as she worked through her last checks and strapped herself into the pilot's chair. Then she flicked on the external monitors to check on Charlie Team and almost jumped out of her skin.

"Shit," she said. "Mechs, loads of them," she yelled over her shoulder. She could hear Muller banging around behind her; then Fernandez floated into the flight deck and strapped himself into the co-pilot's chair.

"What are our options, York?" he asked calmly.

"Bringing the targeting computer and the gun turrets online now, sir," said York, forcing her voice to stay calm. She tapped at the displays, one eye on the view outside, where Mechs were spewing into the bay like ants swarming from a nest.

"Douglas is strapped in, but they'll never make it across that," said Muller from the rear. "The Mechs'll cut them down as soon as they leave the airlock."

"Kearney, you there?" said York.

"Yeah, just trying to work out what to do next," said Kearney.

"The Mechs are heading for us, I think, so sit tight and wait for the signal," said York, "then get ready to move. We're coming to you."

"Roger that," said Kearney. "What's the signal?"

York ignored her, fingers tapping as the targeting computer did its work. "Shit, this thing's slow," she muttered, shaking her head. "Come on, come on," she said, as if she could will it to run any faster.

Outside, the Mechs floated across the bay, weapons at the ready. York watched them, then took another look at the computer. "Nope, too slow," she said a few second later. "Manoeuvring thrusters in five seconds. Hold on, Kearney, we're coming to you."

"Negative, Midshipman," said Fernandez as he looked at the flight plan York was creating. "You haven't seen what those things can do to a ship. They'll cut right through the hull and that'll be the end."

York nodded, but she wasn't really listening.

"York," snapped Fernandez, now alarmed as the manoeuvring thrusters fired, nudging *Stockton* away from her mooring.

The Mechs were close, only twenty metres away, as *Stockton* nudged back and up. "They'll glide straight past, sir," said York smugly as *Stockton* floated clear of the oncoming stream.

"And what about those ones?" said Fernandez, pointing at a dozen Mechs that were approaching from the other side of the bay. "What do we do about them?"

The targeting computer, designed to handle small numbers of large, slow-moving enemy vessels, pinged to say that it had completed its initial scan. "Finally," said York. "And here's your answer, sir," she said, giving the computer permission to open fire.

For half a second, nothing happened. Then there were clunks from beneath and above the ship.

"That's the railgun turrets deploying," said York, "and firing," she added as a rhythmic chatter reverberated throughout the ship.

The targeting computer was as old as the rest of *Stockton*, but age hadn't dulled its ability to prioritise and deal with threats. Fernandez and Muller did little more than watch as York gently eased *Stockton* around the bay, keeping her away from the inner walls as the computer picked off the Mechs. The number of outstanding threats tracked by the targeting computer was falling fast, but so was the amount of ammunition left in the railgun magazines.

"It's going to be close," said York as the ammunition counters spun rapidly down. But then the flow of Mechs into the bay abruptly stopped, and seconds later the rate of fire began to slow as the guns worked their way through the targets.

"Nice work, Midshipman," said Lieutenant Fernandez as first one, then the other railgun fell silent. Dead Mechs floated across the bay, littering *Orion*'s interior with rapidly freezing fluids and body parts.

"Thank you, sir," said York. The ammunition counters showed only a dozen rounds remaining as she guided *Stockton* towards the airlock, rolling the ship to bring the door around to face Charlie Team.

"That's your cue, Kearney," said Fernandez, "it doesn't get any better."

Charlie Team didn't need to be told twice. Hunter and Mason pushed off from the airlock, aimed right at *Stockton*, and flew across the void. Kearney was right behind them and, two minutes later, all three troopers had cycled through the airlock into *Stockton*'s now quite crowded interior.

"That's it, we're in," said Kearney as she joined Hunter, Mason and the others.

"Let's go home," said York, firing the manoeuvring thrusters to spin *Stockton* to face the broad hole in *Orion*'s hull.

"Incoming," warned Fernandez as the manoeuvring thrusters fired, prodding the little craft gently forward. "More Mechs, lots of them."

Mechs were again launching into the bay, but they weren't heading for *Stockton*. "They're going for the hole," said York, "they're trying to cut us off."

"Can we get there before them?" said Fernandez, trying to work out the flight plan in his head.

"Or just shoot them," said Muller, "buy us some time."

"Firing now," said York, as the railguns spun up and chewed through the rest of their magazines. The manoeuvring thrusters completed their program, lining *Stockton* up with *Orion*'s still-open bay doors and slowing the ship to a gentle halt.

But the Mechs still flowed, undeterred by Stockton's brief burst of fire. York watched for a few seconds, breathing deeply. Then she gave a little nod. "Here goes nothing," she said quietly.

"Wait, what?" said Fernandez, alarm once again plastered across his face. "I thought you had a plan?"

Then York fired the main engines, and *Stockton* rocketed forwards, blasting through the thin screen of Mechs and ripping them apart. Mechs bounced off *Stockton*'s hull and careened away into the void.

Fernandez hardly had time to yell before the engines fired *Stockton* through the great hole in *Orion*'s hull and out into the void.

"Woohoo!" said Muller. "That's what I call flying!"

"*Vengeance*," said York, opening a channel with a huge grin on her face, "this is *Stockton*. We're coming home."

"Welcome, *Stockton*. The kippers are waiting."

16

"Target One is accelerating and moving to attack, sir," said Lieutenant Yau. "At the current rate, she'll be in firing range in a little under seven minutes."

There was a moment of tension on the bridge as the crew shuffled uncomfortably in their seats and all eyes turned towards the admiral. Vernon looked at Stansfield, then glanced meaningfully at the battered and battle-damaged bridge. *Vengeance* was in no shape to fight, and they both knew it.

But *Target One* wasn't going to give them the time they needed to prepare.

"This is it," said Stansfield to the bridge. "I know this has been a long day and that we've suffered many setbacks, but now is the time to prove our mettle. We stand at the end of a long line of heroes: Drake, Nelson, Cartwright. And today, our test has arrived. Today we prove ourselves worthy to put our names alongside theirs. This day," said Stansfield, pausing to look around the bridge, his gaze resting on each of the crew in turn, "we fight our Trafalgar, and there is nowhere I would rather be than right here, and no people I would rather have at my side than you." He paused to look around again at the tired, grim faces of the crew. Then he nodded. "Let's get this done."

The bridge came alive as the crew resumed work, and the atmosphere became noticeably more positive. *Vengeance* might be battered and broken, smashed to pieces and lacking reinforcements or backup, but she was still in the game.

"Status reports, please," said Stansfield.

"Weapon systems inoperable, sir," said Midshipman Pickering. "Railgun batteries are offline; missile and torpedo launchers are not available, and our defensive capabilities are largely symbolic."

The atmosphere took a distinct turn towards the dark side as Pickering spoke. Everyone knew things were bad, but laying it out in such stark terms left no room for doubt or hope.

"Symbolic?" said Vernon weakly.

"Ay, sir. The systems are present," said Pickering in an apologetic tone, "but they don't have power. We can't even arm or load, let alone fire."

"And the good news, Midshipman?" said Vernon.

"The targeting computers are online, sir," said Pickering, "and they're getting enough information from the sensors to track and identify local threats, but that's about it."

"So we can pick our targets, but not shoot them?" said Stansfield.

Pickering nodded sadly. "Yes, sir. Sorry, sir."

"Anything else?" said Stansfield.

"Main engines are still offline, sir," said Midshipman Kotter at the helm. "But the hyperspace engine is running through its start-up procedure, and it looks as if the reserve power will be enough for a short trip."

"A rare piece of good news," muttered Stansfield.

"How short?" said Vernon suspiciously.

"Blink and you'd miss it, sir," said Pickering. "Maybe a few light seconds. No more."

"Better than nothing," said Stansfield.

"Yes, sir. And some of the port manoeuvring thrusters are functional," Kotter went on, "but with no more than twenty per cent power. They're also locked in position."

Stansfield snorted. "Which will be useful if we ever need to move slowly sideways."

He looked at Midshipman Campbell. "Comms are working, sir," Campbell said, "but aside from our teams on *Orion* and the Battle Sphere, there's nobody to talk to."

"No improvement in the sensors, sir," said Lieutenant Yau before Stansfield could comment on Campbell's report. "I'm afraid we'll need to physically replace the degraded units to achieve any meaningful improvement."

"Sub-Lieutenant Warburton," said Stansfield, "what news from your department?"

There was a pause before Warburton came online, and when she spoke she sounded stressed and tired.

"Well, there's no chance of getting the main engines working today, sir," she said, "and we've only got a trickle of power from the reserve generators, most of which is being fed to the life support systems. We'll have power to torpedo tube four in a few minutes, but that's the only improvement you'll see anytime soon."

"What if we divert power from life support?" said Vernon. "Would that buy us anything?"

There was another pause. "The life support systems are barely functioning. If we divert power to other systems," Warburton said, in the clear, precise tones of a much put-upon subordinate explaining things she thought were obvious to people who ought to know better, "we'll have only a little time before the air becomes stagnant and we all suffocate, and some parts of the ship, like the bridge, will get uncomfortably warm very quickly."

"But would it give us enough power to do anything useful?" persisted Stansfield.

"More useful than breathe?" said Warburton, before realising she may have gone too far. "No, not really. There's not enough power going to life support to feed the engines or make a difference to the hyperspace drive, and we'd need to lay cables to take power to any of the other systems."

Stansfield took a deep breath. "Thank you, Warburton," he said finally. "Carry on." He closed the channel and shook his head slowly.

"Torpedo tube four just came online, sir," reported Midshipman Pickering. "Loading now, ready to fire in thirty seconds."

"Welcome news," muttered Stansfield as he stared at the main display. He turned the reports over in his mind, but *Vengeance* was a sitting duck. There was nothing he could think of that might make any difference to the forthcoming encounter, but he could at least update the team on the Battle Sphere.

"Get hold of Conway," he said to Vernon. "Let her know what's going on."

"Roger," said Vernon, opening a channel.

Stansfield stared at the tactical display, but his brooding was interrupted by a door opening, and he looked up to see Lieutenant Woodhall striding onto the bridge. He frowned and glanced at Vernon, but the commander was deep in conversation with Conway.

Woodhall was alone. The lieutenant looked around and then, without acknowledging Stansfield or Vernon, strode to a vacant console and slumped down into a chair.

"Four minutes till *Target One* is in firing range," said Yau. "She's fast."

Woodhall sat up, looking around with sudden interest, taking in the near total lack of activity on the bridge. "Are we taking evasive action?" he snapped. "Or are we just going to sit here?"

The atmosphere on the bridge grew very still, and even quieter. Stansfield stared at Woodhall, his face blank, but his fingers tightened about the arms of his command chair. Then he forced himself to release his grip and he leaned forward slightly, staring at Woodhall.

"Where are Captain Ryan and Lieutenant Fernandez?" he asked carefully. "And the members of Charlie Team I sent to assist with the evacuation?"

"The evacuation is complete," said Woodhall stiffly, twitching his attention from the main display to Admiral Stansfield. "The crew are triple-stacked in the quarters, so conditions will be cramped until relief arrives from the Admiralty. We made excellent progress with food, weaponry and flight vessels. Your bays are much like your accommodation – heaving with equipment."

"And I'm surely grateful for your efforts, Lieutenant," said Stansfield slowly, "but what of Ryan, Fernandez and Charlie Team?"

"You have to understand that things were very confused on *Orion* at the end," Woodhall began. "The situation was deteriorating rapidly, and the Mechs were rampaging through the ship. I'm afraid Charlie Team's presence had little impact on the enemy's progress; they may even have made things worse."

"Lieutenant," said Stansfield calmly, "please do not make me ask my question a third time."

Woodhall stared across the bridge for a moment; then he cleared his throat. "Captain Ryan and Lieutenant Fernandez were unable to reach the bay. Charlie Team failed to secure the ship, and the Mechs took control, blocking all access to the bay." He turned to look directly at the admiral. "Captain Ryan, Lieutenant Fernandez and their teams were lost on *Orion*."

"One hundred and fifty seconds to firing range," said Yau, "and I think *Target One* is focused on the Battle Sphere. Maybe we're not a threat," he said.

Stansfield glared at him, then turned back to Woodhall. "We will talk about this later, Lieutenant," he said firmly.

"I do have some good news," Woodhall blurted. "*Conqueror* will soon be joined by *Defender* on the far side of the portal. The Admiralty has ordered a defensive perimeter deployed around the portal on the Earth side."

"Thank you, Lieutenant," said Stansfield.

"So the Admiralty agrees that no more ships should be sent to this side of the portal?" said Vernon.

"No," said Woodhall. "But until *Kingdom10* has been re-militarised, it's not able to play an active role."

"Gentlemen, I have no need to remind you that the real threat still lies ahead. When the armada finally arrives, they will stretch our resources far past their limits. We know that this enemy can be beaten, but this far out in space, with our supply lines already threatened by the Deathless and no prospect of significant reinforcement, we can't be sure of winning any encounter."

"A defeatist attitude won't help, Admiral," admonished Woodhall, as if the losses of *Orion* and *Colossus* could have been avoided by positive thinking.

Stansfield ignored the comment and turned back to look at the main display. "Lieutenant Yau," he said thoughtfully. "How close will *Target One* get?"

"Ah, it looks like she'll pass within two kilometres of *Orion*, then pass even closer to the Battle Sphere, sir," said Yau, frowning at his display as if he didn't believe the projections.

"And she's not slowing down?"

"No, sir," said Yau. "It looks like she's going to make a fast pass."

Stansfield nodded, a slight grin tweaking his lips. "Miss Pickering, I want a firing solution to put a brace of torpedoes in *Target One*'s path."

"Sir," said Pickering, hands flying across her console as she configured the targeting computer.

"Shouldn't we just let them be?" said Woodhall. "If they're attacking their own ships, doesn't that help us?"

Vernon gave Woodhall a withering look, then continued his conversation with Conway. Stansfield didn't appear to have heard.

"Firing solution ready, sir," said Pickering, "although we've time only to fire once, because the reload mechanisms are running at half-speed."

"Forty-five seconds," said Yau.

"Fire when ready, Miss Pickering," said Stansfield, "and then give it everything we've got with the port manoeuvring thrusters, Mr Kotter. Twenty-second burn."

"Sir," said Kotter, although it was clear from his tone that he had no idea what the admiral was planning.

"But this is nonsense," spluttered Woodhall.

"Torpedo away," said Pickering, "twenty seconds to impact."

"Firing thrusters," said Kotter, "maximum power, twenty seconds."

There was a slight nudge as *Vengeance* began moving gently starboard.

"Here she comes," said Yau, and as one the bridge crew tensed, staring at the display as *Target One* grew from an uninteresting dot into a fast-moving battleship.

"No sign of evasive or defensive action," said Pickering. "Five seconds to impact."

Even Woodhall was silent as they watched the torpedo's progress, a tiny speck against a rapidly-growing battleship that seemed to be coming straight at them.

Stansfield gripped the arms of his chair, unable to shake off the feeling that a collision was imminent. And then there was a flash as the torpedo detonated. *Target One* filled the screen, and then it was gone, blasting past *Vengeance* as if the whole fleet were in pursuit.

"Direct hit," said Pickering. "Front and centre."

"She's firing on the Battle Sphere," said Yau. "Railguns and missiles, wide spread, no obvious pattern."

"Conway!" barked Stansfield. "Conway, can you hear me?"

But from the team on the Battle Sphere, there was nothing more than an ominous silence.

17

"Roger that," said Conway, "understood."

"Good luck, Trooper," said Vernon before he closed the channel.

Conway glanced at Gray, then switched back to the team channel. "Listen up," she said as she motioned for Gray to move. "*Target One* is on her way back, and it looks like she's heading this way."

Gray clambered back into the tunnel, and Conway followed, talking as she went, filling in the details. "Davies, how long till you're able to do anything useful from up there?" she asked.

"I don't know," he snapped, sounding stressed. "And I can't promise anything dramatic."

"Well, do what you can," said Conway. "We're on our way to you; then we're leaving regardless, got it?"

"Roger," said Davies, "now let me work!"

"He's getting twitchy," said Gray after Davies dropped out of the channel. "Do we need to worry?"

"No," said Conway with a confidence she didn't feel, desperately hoping that she was right and seriously worried that she might not be. "Davies will get it done."

"Anything more we can do to help, do you think?" said Gray as she followed the route in her HUD that would take them back to Davies and the control room. She turned back to check on Conway when the trooper didn't respond. Conway had stopped in the narrow passageway. "You okay?"

"Got an idea," said Conway, "but we need to get a bit further from the central network hub, so let's crack on."

"Mysterious," murmured Gray as she forged ahead, moving as fast as she dared through the cramped, dark spaces.

"All will become clear," promised Conway.

"This isn't my idea of fun," said Jackson. He and Ten were patrolling the corridors near the network hub, searching for a way to keep the Mechs occupied and away from Davies. "Feels like something's hunting us."

The Sphere was huge, and noises travelled strangely within its twisted hull. It was impossible to tell how far away the sources were, or exactly where the noises were coming from.

"I reckon that's because something *is* hunting us," said Ten as he eased towards a junction and crouched against the wall, lowering his weapon so that he could edge forward and peek around the corner. "Something big and fast and dangerous, with great talons and huge sharp teeth."

"You're not making me feel any better about the situation," said Jackson.

"We're not dead yet," said Ten absentmindedly as he checked the corridor. "All clear," he said, raising his weapon and sliding around the junction. Jackson followed a few seconds later, sticking close to the wall.

The two Marines moved quickly along the passage, scanning alcoves and side rooms as they went until they reached another junction. From the side corridor came the familiar sound of Mechs marching.

"Ready?" said Ten. Jackson nodded, and the two men rolled

around the corner into the corridor, rifles raised.

"Nothing," said Jackson, confused.

They prowled cautiously forwards, but the hairs were rising on the back of Ten's neck, and after a few metres he paused. "Something's wrong," he muttered, stepping into the shadow of a bulkhead. Jackson glanced around, not seeing anything, then took a matching position on the other side of the corridor. "Conway, you okay?"

"We're fine, Ten," said Conway. "We'll be back with Davies in a few minutes. Why do you ask?"

"I think they're gaslighting us," said Ten, waving at Jackson to begin backing along the corridor. "Pulling us into a killing zone."

"You sure about that?" said Conway dubiously. "It's all been 'charge in shooting' so far."

"I'm not at all sure about it," admitted Ten, "but something doesn't feel right. Take care, Conway. We're going to try something different."

"Roger, good luck. I'll let you know when we reach Davies," said Conway. "Out."

"Back that way," said Ten, taking a few steps towards the junction. He paused to remove a block of plastic explosive and a detonator from his pack. "Hold on a moment," he said as he pressed the explosive into a gap behind a conduit and fitted the detonator. "You got any more plastic?"

"Couple of blocks," said Jackson. "Not enough for anything big."

Ten led the way back down the corridor, re-tracing their route from the network hub. "Keep an eye out for somewhere to plant it," he said.

And then, up ahead, something screamed.

D avies swore at the console and tweaked the settings, then tried again. He'd checked and re-checked, and still it wasn't working properly. He had access to everything, he was sure, but that didn't mean he'd been able to find the right settings or controls.

"Update from *Vengeance*," said Conway, breaking his concentration. "*Target One* – some sort of Mech battleship, according to Vernon – is making an attack run. Three minutes."

"Quiet," snapped Davies. "I'm trying to concentrate."

"Just saying you might like to hurry," said Conway.

"What do you think I've been doing?" said Davies. "Taking a little lie-down before the action? I'm working on it!"

"What's the status?" said Conway.

"I don't have fire control," said Davies angrily. "I've got sensors and targeting, I can designate *Target Six* as a target, but I can't trigger the weapons."

"Keep at it, Davies," said Conway encouragingly, "you've got this."

"I might have if I had a little peace and quiet!"

"Roger that," said Conway. "One hundred and fifty seconds to firing range. Out."

Davies swore again and checked the Sphere's external sensors. Everything was routing through his HUD, and the readouts from the sensors and the interfaces Conway had installed filled his vision. He'd even dulled the sounds of fighting to let him concentrate on the problem at hand, but nothing was helping.

He squeezed his eyes shut to try to improve his concentration, then worked through his notes again.

"Must have missed something," he muttered as he checked the schematic. A helpful countdown appeared in the corner of his HUD, a gift from Conway. Davies swiped it away and focused on the problem.

"That's the targeting system, that's the auto-repair config, that's life support," he said as he searched through the Sphere's internal sub-systems. The Mechs used a strange set of glyphs and icons to manage their systems, some of which were disturbingly familiar. But others were unrecognisable, and Davies had to investigate them each in turn as he searched for the system he needed.

"Waste management, fusion reactor control systems, Mech storage..." He paused, wondering if that was worth investigating. Then he shook his head. "Stick with the plan, numb-nuts," he muttered. "Targeting, life support, engine management."

He worked his way through the list, flicking ever faster at the options as he sought the big red button he imagined would end all their problems. But he reached the end of the list without finding anything. "Shit," he said, banging his head against the wall in frustration. "Missed something."

He flicked back to the top of the list then paused, remembering a piece of advice he'd heard a long time before: 'Solutions hide in plain sight.'

Davies shook his head. That had been a stupid piece of advice when he'd first heard it, and it hadn't improved with age. He closed his eyes and took a few deep breaths, trying to stave off exhaustion.

"Think, Davies," he muttered. "Think! Where would you put the triggers if you were designing a system for a bunch of cybernetic organisms with a highly centralised command and control system?"

A channel opened from Commander Vernon, and Davies found his train of thought derailed yet again.

"Brace for impact," said Vernon.

Impact from what? Davies had time to wonder. Then he remembered the in-rushing *Target One* and Conway's timer. He pulled it back just in time to see the digits drop to zero.

"Shit," he said again. Then a flash of inspiration struck, and a sudden urgency seized him. "Can't be that simple, surely," he muttered to himself.

He flicked into the targeting system and flashed through till he found *Target One*. The battleship was in firing range, charging in with weapons armed and locked onto the Sphere. As Davies watched, the ship launched missiles and her railgun batteries opened fire, spitting huge numbers of projectiles at the Sphere.

He nudged the targeting system, and *Target One* was suddenly outlined in a fierce red box. And there, as if by magic, was the firing trigger.

"Oh, *now* you're a threat," muttered Davies, an evil little grin tweaking the corners of his mouth.

A rumble ran through the Sphere as the first of *Target One's* missiles slammed into the hull, and Davies' grin widened. "You've really lost control, haven't you?" he murmured, sending silent thanks to the designers of the Mechs' system.

He unmuted his mic and focused on his HUD as the floor and walls shook and rattled. "Firing now," he said quietly. He tapped the trigger as *Target One* flashed past the Sphere and disappeared into the void, firing as she sped into the gloom.

But she wasn't fast enough. A beam of green light stabbed out from the Sphere, reaching towards *Target One* as she raced away. For half a second the beam seemed to stroke the battleship; then it died away and *Target One* exploded in a vast release of energy.

For a moment, the Sphere's sensors were overwhelmed, and Davies saw nothing but white. Then the view slowly returned, dark void emerging from the static. Stars still hung in the darkness, and nebulae still painted the background.

But *Target One* was gone.

18

"That's it," said Davies, throwing his hands into the air a few minutes later when Conway and Gray arrived back at the control room. "We're done here, nothing else we can do."

"What do you mean?" said Conway. Apart from a lone pair of patrolling guards, they'd seen no Mechs on the return journey. Figgis and his company had fought off three waves of assaults, but there had been no fourth, and the Marines were on edge as they waited for something to happen. The Sphere was spookily quiet.

"They've burned me out of the system," said Davies. "Looks like something took exception to the loss of *Target One*, and they've gone a bit nuclear on the network to stop us doing anything else. Nothing left but dust and smoke."

In the distance, something boomed, and the Sphere gave a little rumbling shake. The team ignored it; the Sphere had been making strange noises ever since they'd arrived.

"Can you fix it?" said Gray. She held up her hands and took half a step backwards when Davies glared at her. "Just asking," she said hurriedly.

"No, I can't fix it," said Davies testily. "Dust and smoke, you get it? They've torched everything, taken it back to the bare metal, as far as I can tell, all to–" He trailed off, distracted by a piece of foam debris that bumped and rolled across the floor.

Davies frowned, and the others followed his gaze as the foam bounced over a discarded panel and accelerated towards the open door that led to the stairwell.

Then they shared a moment of panicked realisation.

"Hull breach," said Conway, mashing the emergency button in her HUD.

Davies stood up and grabbed his helmet, hastily refitting it as the gentle breeze grew rapidly stronger.

"You seeing this, Conway?" said Ten over the team's channel. "Looks like they're scuttling their own ship."

"What?" yelled Conway, uncertain that she'd heard correctly over the strengthening winds. She and Davies forced their way to the edge of the room, where Gray was already locked against the wall to wait out the buffeting storm. Figgis and his company had also gone to ground, jammed up against bulkheads and equipment racks as the howling gale tore at them and battered them with flying debris.

"I said they're scuttling the ship," Ten shouted. "Looks like they've blown a load of bloody great holes in the hull. The whole thing's coming apart at the seams."

"I can't hear you," said Conway. "There's a hull breach, looks like the Sphere's coming apart."

Further conversation was rendered impossible as the racing atmosphere screeched through the ship on its journey to the void. The winds picked up pieces of debris and thrashed them against the walls and the Marines, adding to the noise.

And then, as quickly as it had begun, the wind died away and the Sphere was suddenly as quiet as the deepest pit. The last pieces of debris fell back to the floor, and Charlie Team were left in the cool of the vacuum.

"Everyone okay?" said Conway, looking from Davies to Gray. Both nodded as they picked themselves up.

"We're still alive," said Ten.

"Probably won't be much longer if we don't get off this bloody ship," said Jackson. "There's a hole in the roof of this corridor, and another in the hull, with nothing but stars to be seen beyond."

"Captain Figgis," said Conway on the command channel, "you there?"

"This is Figgis," said Figgis. "You ready to leave?"

"Yes, sir, we are," said Conway. "We've done what we needed to do, there's no reason to stay longer."

"Then we're coming to you," said Figgis. The other door to the control room opened and Marines, led by Lieutenant Collins, appeared.

"It's that way, isn't it?" said Collins, pointing at the door to the stairwell.

"Yes, sir," said Conway.

"Then let's get moving," said Collins. "You know the way, so you get to take point."

"I don't know the way," muttered Davies, "could I take a turn in the middle?" But Conway slapped him on the shoulder and he stumbled after her, with Gray just behind.

"Ten, we're moving," said Conway. "We'll be at the shuttles in, er, a few minutes."

"Good," replied Ten.

"You sure you're okay?" said Conway as she led the column of Marines out of the control room, eyes flashing as she sought the enemy.

"Let me get back to you on that," said Ten.

Then the Sphere shook, and suddenly there was no time for anything but survival.

"Can you get a line on the bastards?" said Jackson, leaning out around a pile of equipment to peer down the corridor before ducking quickly back as a brace of muzzles flared in the darkness. The wall behind him was already punched through with holes as the Mechs worked to pin down the Marines.

"No," said Ten, who was on the other side of the passage, jammed against the wall and thinking thin thoughts to avoid exposing himself to the Mechs. He held his rifle out and squeezed off a few rounds, then shook his head. "Pointless," he muttered.

"What the hell was that?" said Jackson as the floor rumbled beneath them and part of the ceiling was torn away.

"No fucking idea," said Ten, "but we really need to get off this ship."

"If that's even still possible," said Jackson. "Are we doing this?"

Ten glanced across the corridor. "Live fast, or die trying," he said. "On three?"

"On three," said Jackson.

"One – two – three," said Ten, pushing into the corridor and charging forward. Jackson moved at the same time, scrambling over the equipment he'd been sheltering behind and firing down on the Mechs that huddled only a few metres away.

The Marines worked in silence, moving and firing and moving again, bearing down on the Mechs and forcing them to retreat or take cover. A couple of Mechs fired back, but they were swept away as soon as they appeared from cover, and moments later the corridor was clear. Ten checked the corpses, making sure that the OctoBots were as dead as the host Mechs; then they hurried on along the corridor.

"This ship's no longer safe for human habitation," said Jackson.

They moved more quickly now that there was no atmosphere to carry the sound of their footsteps, but still they checked every room and passage to guard against ambush or attack.

"Couldn't agree more," said Ten, slowing as he reached a junction and peering cautiously around a corner. "But – argh!" He took a step and suddenly found himself weightless and floating up towards the ceiling, exposed in the centre of the crossroads.

"Looks like the artificial gravity's failed," said Jackson.

"You think?" snapped Ten as he put out a hand to steady himself against the ceiling.

"Ten, you at the bay yet?" said Conway.

"Having some trouble with the floor," said Ten as he kicked off the ceiling along the corridor, "but we're on our way."

"Well, hurry it up," said Conway. "We've made it to the bay, and we're not alone."

"Roger, understood," said Ten. "Better get a wiggle on," he said to Jackson, and the two Marines hastened along the corridor, following the route laid out in their HUDs as around them, the Sphere tensed as its structural integrity began to fail.

Stansfield watched the distant armada on the main screen. With *Target One* eliminated and *Target Six* all but dead, *Vengeance* was experiencing a brief moment of peace as the crew worked to restore functions to the stricken vessel.

Each piece of good news was welcomed on the bridge. The news that one of the aft railgun batteries was now online – albeit running at only ten per cent capacity – was greeted by a small cheer.

But Stansfield's energies were focused only on the armada. Lieutenant Yau's threat analysis scrolled across the admiral's data slate and made for depressing reading. Even if *Vengeance* had been in top form and perfect working order, there was no realistic prospect of stopping the armada from doing exactly what it wanted. In her current state, *Vengeance* would be unable even to attract their attention, let alone impede their plans.

Stansfield drummed his fingers on the arm of his chair. The unpalatable truth was that *Vengeance* was irrelevant. The coming encounter wasn't one they could hope to survive, let alone win, but the thought of surrender was no more appealing.

"But if we can't win," muttered Stansfield under his breath, "what choice do I have?" He pondered a little longer, then shook his head. "No choice at all," he murmured, sitting up in his chair and looking around the bridge. "Where's Captain Ryan?" he asked to nobody in particular.

"His shuttle has just arrived, sir," said Midshipman Pickering, "along with the Marines assigned to help Charlie Team."

"Good. Have someone bring them to me."

Stansfield retired to his ready room and resumed his drumming, turning over the idea and peering at it from every direction. "Timing," he muttered, "that'll be the key. If we can just get everything to fall into place."

The door slid open and Captain Ryan entered the room, still wearing his powered armour. But the once-fine suit was now battered and scarred from hard use, banged about and beaten up, much like the man inside. He sat down opposite Stansfield, set his suit helmet on the table and nodded.

"Admiral," he said tiredly. "Good to see you again." Ryan's clone appeared to have aged a decade in the hours since he and Stansfield had first met.

"Captain Ryan," said Stansfield, "you have my deepest sympathies for the loss of your ship and crew, but we're not beaten yet. Is there anything you think we might have missed or overlooked? Anything we could have done differently?"

Ryan looked like a man worn down by the terrors of battle and stretched thin by stress and loss. But his voice was clear when he spoke. "Nothing," he said with a slow shake of his head. "But I want to blast every last Mech into a deep robot grave." He was seething now, like a man on the edge of collapse but hell-bent on revenge.

Stansfield nodded, and the two men shared a look. "In this, we agree," he said.

Then Lieutenant Woodhall appeared, somehow, and took a seat at the end of the table. Ryan and Stansfield stared at him, and it seemed that he was the only person not affected by the events of the day.

"We need to get away while we still can," said Woodhall. "The armada is bearing down on us, and if we wait much longer it'll be too late. If we leave immediately, we can lose ourselves in this system's asteroid belt."

Ryan's eyes glinted with anger as he turned to face Woodhall, but the admiral spoke first.

"You wish to leave? To abandon our people on the Sphere? To take *Vengeance*, the only Royal Navy ship on this side of the portal, the only human vessel within thousands of light years, and leave our post to escape into the darkness where the enemy might no longer be able to find us?"

"Well, yes!" spluttered Woodhall. "We can't beat them! They have hundreds of ships! We have to leave, and the sooner the better. It's our only hope of survival."

"Lieutenant," Ryan growled. Woodhall's confidence seemed to melt away as the captain glared at him, but Stansfield held up a hand and Ryan bit back his words.

"Thank you for your thoughts, Lieutenant," said Stansfield. "I will take them into account." He opened a channel in his HUD. "Lieutenant Yau, Commander Vernon, will you join us in my ready room, please?"

A moment later, the door slid open and Yau and Vernon stepped in. The commander nodded at Ryan, but narrowed his eyes when he saw Woodhall at the other end of the table. He took a seat near Stansfield and settled back to listen.

"Sir?" said Yau, looking around.

"Take a seat, Lieutenant," said Stansfield, "and let me outline my plan."

Yau slipped into the space between Woodhall and Ryan, set a slim data slate on the table before him, and cleared his throat.

"Lieutenant Woodhall counsels flight, for the solid reason that the armada is far too large for us to fight. And he has the ear of the Admiralty, and we are bound to consider his opinion," said Stansfield. Woodhall frowned at this and squirmed in his seat, but he said nothing.

"But we will not be leaving," said Stansfield. Woodhall opened his mouth to object, but the admiral held up his hand. "We will not be leaving, Lieutenant, because *Vengeance* and *Orion* are the only ships between the armada and the portal, and if the Mechs get through–"

"But we can't stop them," said Woodhall. "*Orion*'s a wreck, and *Vengeance* isn't much better. It's impossible!"

"If you interrupt me just once more, Lieutenant," said Stansfield in a cold, calm tone, "I will have your mind state stored and your clone reassigned to someone who will put it to better use. Is that clear?"

Woodhall opened in his mouth and frowned. "I don't think the Admiralty would–"

"Lieutenant!" thundered Stansfield, pushing himself out of his chair to lean on the table, his patience exhausted. "The correct response when given an order by a superior office is 'Yes, sir', and if you can't manage that, then present yourself to the cloning bay for storage!"

Woodhall looked shocked. He blinked. "Yes, sir," he said, nodding meekly, "understood."

Stansfield waited a moment longer, leaning on his fists; then he slowly sank back into his chair. "The destruction of *Target One* and the incapacitation of *Target Six* means that we are safe until the armada arrives," he said, picking up where he'd left off as if Woodhall had never opened his mouth, "but we don't know when they will arrive and, once they're here, our options will dramatically diminish with little hope of recovery."

The faces around the table were grim as Stansfield continued his summary. "*Orion* is beyond recovery, and therein lies our opportunity to snatch victory from the jaws of defeat."

"Opportunity?" said Ryan with a frown.

Stansfield gave an uncomfortable half-smile and shifted in his seat. "We're a long way from home," he said. "We've travelled further than any Royal Navy vessel in history, but the route home is open not only to us, but also to our enemies."

"The portal," said Vernon. His face was ashen.

"The portal," said Stansfield with a nod. "The enemy's greatest strength and their only weak point. Destroy it and we trap them here, years from Sol, where they can't ever do any harm. But if they make it through, if they get to human-inhabited space, they'll do untold damage and might even swing the war with the Deathless against us."

"So we lace the area with explosives, pass through the portal, then trigger the explosives to lock the door behind us," said Ryan, nodding as he understood the nature of the plan. Then the light dawned. "And *Orion* is the explosive, isn't she?"

"She is," said Stansfield. "I'm sorry, Ryan, but we need her self-destruct mechanism to destroy the portal. It's the only option."

Ryan sighed. He looked down at the table for a few seconds, then shook his head. "I don't see another solution," he said quietly, "and if it traps the Mechs here, then it'll be a worthy sacrifice."

"Then we're agreed?" said Stansfield, looking around the table.

Vernon nodded. "No other way," he said.

Ryan looked up, held Stansfield's eyes for a moment, then nodded. "Agreed. There's no other way. I'll make the necessary preparations."

"Lieutenant Yau?" said Stansfield. The Science Officer looked surprised to be consulted, then he too nodded.

"Yes, sir," he said. "It's the only way."

"Then we're unanimous," said Stansfield. "Let's make it happen as soon as possible, then we can put this behind us." He stood up, and all but Woodhall followed.

"Well, I don't agree," said Woodhall, who seemed to have recovered his nerve. "And the Admiralty surely won't approve this course of action!"

Stansfield turned and gave Woodhall a cold, thin smile. "Noted, Lieutenant, but we're long past playing games. It's time for the final push, and you need to decide if you're with us, or against us."

Woodhall frowned and looked from Stansfield to Ryan.

"Well, Lieutenant?" said Stansfield. "Which is it to be?"

∾

"They're all over the place," said Davies as he fired on the Mechs that were clustering on the far side of the bay. Some were already mounted on discs and heading for the doors, but most were waiting in line or taking potshots at the Marines.

"Are they abandoning the Sphere?" said Conway as squad after squad of Mechs disappeared through the open doors to the relative safety of the void. Both sides, it seemed, were intent on evacuating the Sphere.

"Looks like it," said Davies as he reloaded his rifle, "but they're taking their sweet time about it."

Behind them, Figgis' Marines were filing from the Sphere into one of the waiting shuttles as the flight crew bustled around to get them loaded and stowed.

"Where the hell is Ten?" snapped Davies as he and Conway traded shots with the Mech guards on the other side of the bay. Their rifles' recoil kept trying to push them clear of their cover, nudging at them as they fired; fighting in zero-G was no joke.

"Above and beyond," said Ten cryptically. "We're on our way, but the Mechs are everywhere, and they're all heading the same way as us."

"They're evacuating," said Conway, "like rats from a sinking ship."

"Well, they're between us and you," said Ten, "so if you've got any ideas, now would be the time."

"Fly away on the shuttle and leave you to your fate?" said Conway. "Look, there're two shuttles. We're taking one, the other is closer to you, and we can't get to it. The flight crew are with us, though, and there's no way to get them back to their ship; is that going to be a problem?"

"You're taking our flight crew?" said Jackson. "Nope, can't see a problem with *that*, not at all."

"I can fly it," said Ten. "Get out of there, Conway. You've done all you need to do."

"Are you sure?" said Conway. The last thing she wanted to do was abandon Ten and Jackson.

"Go," said Ten firmly. "We've got this."

"Roger," said Conway. "Thanks, Ten."

"You rigged the central hub to blow, right?" said Ten. "Now might be a good time to flick the switch."

"Roger that, can't do any harm," said Conway. "Detonation in three – two – one. Done. Any obvious effect?"

"Nothing so far," said Ten, "except a slight rumble in the walls."

"Oh, and now the lights have gone out," said Jackson. "Just when I thought things couldn't get any worse, now we have to escape in the dark. Thanks, Conway."

19

York threw the ancient fighter-bomber *Stockton* towards *Vengeance* with all possible speed. The tiny craft twisted, manoeuvring thrusters firing as soon as she was clear of *Orion*'s hull, and the main engines kicked in again. *Stockton* accelerated, burning fast towards the safety of the battleship and pressing the crew into their seats.

"Four minutes left," said York, her voice strained as the acceleration crushed her chest. "Hold on."

Groans floated forward from the tiny compartment where Charlie Team and the Marines were crowded together. Despite the pain and discomfort, York grinned as the Marines muttered the familiar insults and complaints.

"Stop whining," she shouted, knowing that the Marines wouldn't take the slightest notice of her command, "we'll be safe on *Vengeance* in ten minutes." More complaints; nobody believed *Vengeance* was a refuge, not any more.

"It is a bit uncomfortable," said Fernandez from across the cramped flight deck.

"It's a short period of discomfort, sir," said York, "or a long period of being dead."

Before Fernandez could respond, the main engines switched off as *Stockton* completed the first part of the flight. The manoeuvring thrusters fired briefly, flipping *Stockton* end over end; then the main engines fired again as the ship began to decelerate towards *Vengeance*.

"Ah, that's the business," murmured York, eyes closed as she was again pressed into her seat.

"Funny," said Fernandez, "the damage doesn't look so bad from out here."

York opened her eyes. The monitors showed *Orion* hanging against the stars, lit by the light of the distant stars and sparkling in the dark. "I loved that ship," she said sadly. "What's *Vengeance* like?"

Fernandez snorted. "Even before the Mechs arrived, she was held together by spit and luck. Now? I dread to think."

"On the plus side," said York, "it probably won't be our problem for much longer."

Fernandez twisted his head to look at York, a movement that took an inordinate amount of effort. "You're not the comfort you think you are, York," he said.

"*Stockton*, this is *Vengeance*," said a voice before York could reply. "You're cleared to dock, if that's even still possible given your velocity. We're ready for you; medical teams are standing by. You're to report to the bridge once you've crashed."

"You mean 'landed', surely, *Vengeance*?" said York.

"Yeah, right, whatever you say, *Stockton*. Good luck. *Vengeance* out."

York ran her eyes over the flight plan, but things were changing too fast for her to get a handle on the situation. "I guess we'll just have to see," she muttered.

She closed her eyes again and concentrated on the physical act of dragging air into her lungs. Then a warning sounded and her eyes snapped open. The display had switched from the view of *Orion* to a non-descript patch of space.

"What the hell?" she muttered, frowning at the display. It flashed again, zooming in, and a Mech battleship appeared against the backdrop, newly arrived and as welcome as a kick in the teeth. "Oh, shit," she said.

"I think that's probably the end of our little escape attempt," said Fernandez. A second battleship appeared, then a third, then a whole flurry more, and suddenly the screen was thick with enemy ships of more sizes and shapes than York could count.

"*Vengeance*, are you seeing this?" she said.

"The huge enemy armada on our doorstep? Yes, *Stockton*," said a testy voice from *Vengeance*, "we had noticed them. Suggest you get aboard unless you have a solution. *Vengeance* out."

"You heard the man," said Fernandez. "Let's see what the admiral's planning to do about it."

~

"Admiral, we have a situation developing," said Pickering as Stansfield and the others emerged from the ready room. "Placing a visual on the main screen now."

The armada of enemy ships was appearing at the point where the battleships had previously arrived. Ship after ship appeared, piling out of hyperspace in a neat formation, all facing *Orion* and the portal.

"So much for having time to prepare," said Vernon quietly.

"How are they doing this, Pickering?" Stansfield demanded. "We should have had hours, at least, to prepare!"

"Some sort of hyperspace drive, I guess, sir," said Pickering weakly. "Sorry."

The bridge crew could only watch as the battleships broke formation and began to manoeuvre.

"Looks like they're moving to secure the portal," said Lieutenant Yau.

"Secure it from what?" muttered Vernon.

"Are they launching fighters?" said Ryan. "There, from that vessel amongst the battleships." He pointed at a single vessel shaped like a huge cigar, from which smaller ships were spewing.

"Could be fighters, sir," said Yau. "Or possibly small troop transports."

"Or gunboats or torpedo carriers or lifeboats, for all we know," snapped Stansfield.

"They're heading for the portal," said Yau, hands flying over his console. Flight paths appeared on the main display, a thick cord of yellow linking the carrier vessel to the portal as the newly released ships accelerated. Four squadrons of enemy ships passed through the portal over the next few minutes as the bridge crew watched, unable to intervene.

"That's the fifth squadron," Pickering reported as another group of ships passed through the portal. "And there's the sixth lining up."

"Open a channel to *Conqueror*," said Stansfield. "I want to know what those ships are up to."

"This is *Conqueror*," said a voice a few moments later. "Lieutenant Elson speaking."

"This is Admiral Stansfield. I want to know what's happening on your side of the portal, Lieutenant. What are those ships doing?"

There was a pause. "Er, they're, ah, well," said the lieutenant. There was another pause before she spoke again. "The first three squadrons are heading towards *Kingdom 10*, sir, and the rest are assuming an attack formation on a wide perimeter around *Conqueror*."

A second voice interrupted Elson's report. "This is Captain Pierce of HMS *Conqueror*. To whom am I speaking?"

"This is Admiral Stansfield of HMS *Vengeance*," said Stansfield. "Good to make your acquaintance, Captain."

"Likewise, sir," said Pierce. "The situation here is becoming confused. Are these ships a threat, sir?"

"Very much so, Captain," said Stansfield. "They will certainly attempt to capture or destroy *Kingdom 10* if given the opportunity, and I don't doubt that *Conqueror* will be next."

"In that case, I will take the necessary steps," said Pierce. "Is there anything you require from *Conqueror*, Admiral?"

"Thank you, Captain, but there's nothing you can do for us at the moment," said Stansfield.

"Very good," said Pierce. "In that case, if you'll excuse me, I have an enemy to engage."

"Happy hunting, Captain."

"And good luck to you too, Admiral," said Piece. "*Conqueror* out."

"Two more squadrons forming up," said Pickering.

"This has to be it, Ed," said Stansfield, speaking quietly and directly to his number two. "There's too much movement now, they're taking their final positions."

"Agreed," said Vernon, "and we're stuck in this bloody box without a thing we can do to defend ourselves."

"Where are Charlie Team?" snapped Stansfield to the bridge.

"Hunter, Mason and Kearney are with Fernandez, sir," said Yau. "They'll be docking any time now."

"Conway and Davies?" said Vernon.

"On the Sphere, or what's left of it," said Yau. "With Captain Figgis and a company of Marines. They were evacuating, last we'd heard, but comms have been intermittent."

"Get hold of them, Lieutenant," said Vernon, "and find out when they'll be back on *Vengeance*."

"Aye, sir, working on it," said Yau.

"That pulsing's getting louder," complained Vernon. "Or is it just that it's becoming more annoying?"

Stansfield grunted. The pulsing had been going on so long that he'd almost forgotten it entirely. Then there was a flash of white light from behind the enemy ships, and everybody on the bridge turned towards the screens to see what had caused it.

"Scanning," said Pickering, her hands battering her console. "It wasn't an explosion. Something just jumped through space, another ship, a big one."

The main display flashed as the forward sensors focused on the new arrival. An image appeared of a huge vessel, flanked by battleships and three more of the vast cigar-shaped carriers. It sat there behind the Mech fleet like a monstrous carbuncle.

"What the hell is that?" said Vernon.

But Stansfield nodded. "It's her," he said simply.

Vernon's head whipped around. "How do you know?"

"Who else could it be, Ed?" said Stansfield. "And did you notice the pulsing? It stopped right at the moment her vessel arrived. It's her all right, and now it's time to see what she wants."

Vernon nodded.

"Time to brief the team," said Stansfield, pushing himself from his seat and looking like he'd aged another decade. "We've kept this secret too long already."

20

"It's time to come clean, Admiral," said Davies. His avatar hung on the display in the admiral's ready room, but his voice boomed from the speakers, and he spoke with the carefree abandon of someone under heavy enemy fire.

Vernon had pulled Davies and Conway into a hastily convened briefing, along with Captain Pierce of *Conqueror*. Davies and Conway showed only as static images, but Pierce sat in his own ready room on *Conqueror*, smartly turned out and with a mug of coffee on the table before him. Lieutenants Yau and Fernandez had joined Commander Vernon and Admiral Stansfield, and Lieutenant Woodhall had been summoned.

"When I linked to the data area on *Vengeance*, I came across a Tombstone," said Davies. "There are elements of all missions that have to remain secret, but there's a lot at stake here, Admiral. If we're going to resolve this situation, we need to know the truth."

Stansfield nodded. In a short amount of time he'd already come to respect Davies' immense talents, and if he'd discovered the Tombstone, then he already knew more than he should. He glanced at Vernon, who held his gaze, then nodded.

"I think it's probably time," said Vernon. "Now she's here."

Stansfield looked around the group, and when he next spoke, his tone was heavy and serious, as if all the life had been drained from him. "What I'm about to tell you must remain confidential," he said. "Not just today. This information is classified at the very highest level and is never likely to be declassified. Is that clear? Do you understand the implications and what you surrender by remaining in this conference?"

He looked around the room again, checking that everyone had heard and understood before proceeding. Lieutenants Yau and Fernandez shuffled uncomfortably, but Captains Ryan and Pierce seemed much more relaxed.

"It pertains to information that Davies uncovered while accessing the files on *Vengeance* – and we can talk about exactly how he found them later," Stansfield said as an aside, "but to be truthful, we've been biding our time before making this information known to the Admiralty."

And now he had their complete attention.

"As you will know, a small volunteer team from *Vengeance* was placed in stasis just beyond the location of the portal, over a hundred and ten years ago. *Kingdom 10* was built as an outpost in this part of space shortly after, and her purpose was to support the crew of *Vengeance* with whatever was coming."

There was an uneasy shuffling around the table. The construction of a dedicated support outpost suggested a worrying degree of foresight.

"You'd met this enemy before?" blurted Davies.

"We had," said Vernon with a slow nod. "They were the last enemy we fought before entering our deep sleep."

Stansfield paused, figuring out how to sequence the story's events. Then the door opened and Lieutenant Woodhall strode in, tugging at his uniform as if to disguise the fact that he'd been running.

"Take a seat, Lieutenant," said Stansfield coldly. "And keep your mouth shut."

Woodhall opened his mouth, but the expression on the admiral's face was clear, even to him, and he sank silently into a chair.

Stansfield glared at him until he was sure the lieutenant had understood his instructions; then he turned to face the room and continue his briefing.

"The nice, well-ordered galaxy you know today was once very different," said Stansfield, as if he were giving a lecture in modern history. "More volatile, more dangerous, less well-governed. There was a great deal of unrest in the centuries after the Warming. You know about the Ark ships, of course. Thousands of the damned things were launched, and we're paying for that in our war with the Deathless, though I hope to retire before we're dragged into that particular squabble."

"You and me both," muttered Conway, speaking more freely than she might have normally. "It's one of the reasons Charlie Team got stranded without clone backups so deep in space. There's only so long you can do what we do, and we've had enough."

"Understandable," said Stansfield. "Warfare can be a brutal master. I wouldn't wish it upon my greatest enemy," he said, with not a hint of irony.

"So, how come we're all here?" said Davies, keen not to lose the thread. He'd pieced much of it together, but he needed to know how much he'd got right.

"I'm out," said Conway suddenly, and for a few seconds the officers could only listen as Charlie Team organised their escape from the Sphere.

The admiral waited for silence. "I negotiated with the Commonwealth at the very highest levels that *Vengeance* should be the ship that responded when the portal eventually re-opened," he said. "Prior to its final opening, we were led to this part of space in a chase. A covert operations team from a hostile Ark ship had infiltrated a remote Admiralty science station to steal a series of top-secret files. Those files held the latest breakthroughs on wormholes, hyperspace technology and cybernetics."

"But not cloning?" interrupted Davies. "I'm guessing that didn't include cloning, or else the Mechs would still be human."

"But not cloning," confirmed Vernon. "Full-body cloning was in its infancy and very tightly controlled, locked down to a few locations on Earth. Besides, the Ark ship was packed with some of the Commonwealth's best engineers and scientists. It was a massive blow. Who knows how many years it set us back? If they'd stayed on Earth, we may well have had wormholes that could transport ships by now."

There was an awkward silence. Then Vernon cleared his throat. "Two more squadrons are heading for the portal," he said.

Captain Pierce waved a hand. "Merely probing," he said confidently. "They're getting nowhere. We have this under control, and *Defender* will soon arrive to reinforce us."

"Maybe things are finally going our way," said Vernon, although from his tone he clearly didn't believe it. "Do you want me to take the bridge?"

"Stay a little longer, Ed. I want you to be involved in this. I need your input. I'm sure Captain Pierce will let us know if his situation changes."

"Of course, Admiral," said Pierce.

Stansfield nodded. "The Ark ship was led by a brilliant engineer and scientist. Did you know that my own background is in high-energy particle physics and containment engineering?" said the admiral, looking around the table. "Well, it is. As a young man, I was quite involved in exploratory work to create wormholes and jump technology. The Commonwealth believed that if we could master that technology, it would hasten our supremacy in space and help defend us from future attack.

"I worked with the engineer who went on to guide that Ark ship away from Earth. We were both members of a team working on cutting-edge technology, ideas that would power our civilisation forward. It was serious, important work, and we were excited to play our part."

For a moment, Stansfield sounded truly alive, as if he were

reliving the excitement of his youth. Then he sighed and seemed to collapse back into himself.

"But we pushed too far. We chased our dreams too hard, took too many risks, cut one corner too many in our desperate race to succeed." Now Stansfield looked positively deathly, and his voice fell to a near whisper. "We thought we'd done it. Thought we'd mastered the portal technology, that we had solved all the problems. But there was massive fallout after one of our tests went wrong, after so many people died."

The room was silent as the watching officers waited for the admiral to compose himself.

"It was the biggest error of judgement I ever made," Stansfield said finally, steadying his voice. "It was also the reason I moved to active service in the military and turned my back on engineering."

Vernon put his arm on Stansfield's shoulder. There was a strong sense of friendship between the two men; they weren't just sharing command, they had serious history. They were like brothers.

"We were testing breakthrough portal technology," said Stansfield. "The ability to send battleships thousands of light years across space. That was the goal. I was younger, more impetuous, but too young and too inexperienced to lead a major research project. We set up a test, but Phoenix – the head engineer – refused to take part. She said we were reckless, ill-prepared. The arguments dragged on for months as we made the preparations. She warned us over and over. She said the portal was unsafe, that more work was needed, that we shouldn't send any ships through it.

"But we didn't listen. We ignored her warnings, determined to snatch our prize. Too soon. We sent a shuttle full of observers, scientists and technicians through the portal. A short hop to prove the system," said Stansfield, now oblivious to the updates that were coming over the comms.

"Volunteers, all of them, and as eager as I was to prove the technology. We'd done tests, so may tests. We – I – was certain it was safe, that we had done all that could be done." He fell silent, staring down at the table.

"What happened, sir?" said Captain Ryan.

Stansfield looked up and drew a ragged breath. "Phoenix left before the test, took flight on an Ark ship. We went ahead, but the portal wasn't stable. It was far too soon for a live trial, but just being part of something so big, so important, drove us on."

Stansfield's eyes were red and close to tears. Even though he'd been in stasis for over a century, this was still a raw wound for the admiral.

"The shuttle was lost as it crossed the portal," he said in a voice so low it was barely audible. "Shredded in a catastrophic failure with all lives lost. I had been so certain, and that certainty cost the lives of every one of our people on the shuttle. The project was shut down immediately, and the teams dispersed."

The near silence was broken only by background noise from Conway's comms as Charlie Team completed their evacuation of the Sphere.

Stansfield rubbed his eyes and cleared his throat. "The armada before us was built by the engineers who left with Phoenix on that Ark ship. The incredible engineering, the intellect required to achieve everything that you've seen, could all have been Sol's if we hadn't been so pig-headed, if we hadn't chased Phoenix and her teams away. And now she's back to claim what's hers. She's returned to Earth for her revenge. She's come back to punish me."

"But why?" said Conway. "Why now? Why you? What does she gain in a fight with Sol? What's in it for her?"

"You have to understand," said Stansfield, pleading. "To the Navy, it was just an accident. A dreadful, horrible accident, but an accident nonetheless. Test pilots and their teams have been taking risks for centuries. Millennia, even. But Phoenix and her teams were side-lined, and she felt betrayed by me. I thought the portal was ready, I made sure she was overruled. I thought she'd understand when it worked; I thought she'd see her error and come back to the project."

"But why is she so angry, sir?" said Conway, pushing the point.

Stansfield said nothing, and an awkward filled the room until the admiral finally spoke again. "Because Phoenix was my wife," he said eventually, "and I gave our only son permission to fly on the test vessel. Encouraged him. I was so certain, I was so sure it was safe, that I allowed my own son, at the beginning of his military career, to take the test flight. He perished with the others, and Phoenix never forgave me."

He looked up at the display that showed the approaching armada. "Still hasn't forgiven me, it seems. And now she's here for revenge."

21

"Are you sure it's this way?" said Jackson doubtfully. "This isn't looking familiar."

Ten paused and looked at the walls, floor and ceiling of the corridor they were in. With the lights out, they dared not move too fast for fear of ambush, and they were using only the dimmest of lamps to avoid giving away their position. Not that there were many Mechs left; they seemed to be leaving the Sphere in droves, and it had been some time since the two Marines had even seen one.

"Yeah, you might be right," said Ten, catching onto the wall and turning himself around. "Maybe we should have turned left at that last junction."

"Ten, Jackson," said Conway on the shared channel. "Are you ever going to get to the bay?"

"We're taking the scenic route," snapped Ten.

"Okay, no need to snap," said Conway. "But the bay's hot with Mechs and the sooner you get here, the better."

"Why are you still here?" said Ten, changing the subject as he and Jackson backtracked to the previous junction and took the other turning. "I thought you were taking the shuttle back to *Vengeance*."

"We're finishing up the load, but Stansfield's called some sort of conference, and I don't want to have to report that we left you behind, so hurry it up, will you?"

"Much as I want to avoid inconveniencing the admiral," said Ten, pausing briefly to peer into another dark room, "things are a trifle difficult out here."

"Just don't hang around," said Conway. "Out."

"This looks good," said Jackson as they turned into a new corridor. The skimmed along the walls, one on either side of the passage. At the end, a heavy door waited for them.

"Locked," said Ten as he banged on the controls, "or out of power. Either way, it ain't gonna open."

"I don't want to hang around here waiting for the Sphere to fall apart," said Jackson, "so maybe it's time for the magic plasticine." He pulled a pressurized tube of plastic explosive from his pack and ripped it open.

Ten nodded. "Good one. Hinges, do you think, or right through the middle?"

Jackson eyed the door. "I reckon this one slides," he said, "so we'll go right through the middle. Keep an eye out," he said as he set to work. "Nice little bang-bang worms," he muttered as he squirted explosive onto the surface of the door, marking out a neat section large enough for the Marines to squeeze through. "Better hope it's the bay on the other side," he said. "This is the last of my supply."

From along the corridor a sudden light flickered, and they both froze.

"Shit," murmured Jackson, turning quickly back to his work as Ten braced himself against the wall and peered back along the passage. The light flashed again, absurdly bright in the near-total darkness.

"Yup, we've got company," said Ten. "Work faster."

"Almost done," said Jackson as he closed the circle. He produced a detonator, keyed it to his HUD, then pressed it into the explosive. "Done."

"Firing," said Ten as he squeezed off a few rounds at whatever was lurking in the dark at the end of the corridor. "Mechs of some sort, no idea what."

"Just move," said Jackson from a few metres down the side passage, where he was sheltering behind a buttress. "Let's blow this and get out of here."

Ten fired again, then moved the other way, slipping into cover and turning away to shield his eyes. "Go."

"And bang," said Jackson as he triggered the detonator. The explosive fired, brighter than a young sun in the gloom of the Sphere, and when Jackson looked back, there was a neat hole right through the door. Starlight from the open bay doors shone through the hole and into the corridor to illuminate the Mechs that still filled the space.

"Move," said Ten, sliding out of cover to peer back along the corridor. "Mechs!" he yelled, firing into the group that hung only a few metres away, apparently overwhelmed by the brightness of the explosion.

Ten fired repeatedly, drilling each of the Mechs in turn, emptying his magazine and hurriedly slotting in a new one as Jackson looked through the gap in the door.

"All clear," said Jackson, "time to go."

Some of the Mechs were firing, now, spraying rounds into the corridor, filling it with fire and hitting their own side more than they inconvenienced the Marines.

"Come on," said Jackson, firing to cover Ten as he reloaded. "Go!"

"Get through there," said Ten, nodding at the hole and firing into the mass of Mechs. Jackson didn't hang around to be told a second time. He squeezed into the hole and pulled himself through into the bay, then fired back over Ten's shoulder.

"Come on!" he shouted, slinging his rifle and waving.

Ten moved towards the hole, floating backwards as he fired at the Mechs. Then he turned and dived through the hole, arms outstretched. The Mechs opened fire, and bullets clanged off every surface as Jackson grabbed him and pulled him through into the bay.

"Where's the fucking shuttle?" shouted Ten as he hung by the gaping hole in the door and reloaded his rifle. Light poured in through the open bay doors, making the enormous space feel somehow unreal. The Mechs poured fire through the hole, and Ten tossed a couple of grenades back at them.

"I think it's that thing over there," said Jackson doubtfully, pointing at a shuttle only a few dozen metres away.

"Seriously?" said an incredulous Ten. "Doesn't *Vengeance* have anything nice, or do we just get all the shit things?" The shuttle sat next to a ramp, doors closed. The lights were off, and it looked like it hadn't moved in years. The ship's name – *Linthorpe* – was stencilled in faded letters on the hull, amidst the scratches and dents that spoke of a long working life.

"Ten, Jackson," said Conway suddenly. "Get your arses on that shuttle and get out of there."

Ten spun around, searching the bay until he saw the second shuttle on the far side. Between them and Conway was a whole cluster of Mechs, and as he watched some of them turned, noticing the new arrivals.

"Shit," said Ten, "time to go." Jackson pushed off from the wall, heading toward the dormant shuttle, and Ten followed quickly, glancing back over his shoulder at the door. "Enemies behind," he warned as a Mech floated through the hole.

"This isn't going to work," said Jackson as he reached the shuttle. He flipped around to face the door, unslung his rifle, and began to fire at the Mechs as they emerged through the hole.

"Stop fucking around," snapped Ten as he landed on the shuttle and searched for the access controls. He found them, and the door slid open. "Get in here," he said, unslinging his own rifle to cover Jackson's retreat. The Mechs returned fire as more and more of them emerged from the hole in the door.

"Definitely time to go," said Ten as Jackson reached the shuttle's airlock. "Hold them off, right? I'll get us moving," he said. Then he swung around and hauled himself through the ship, heading for the cockpit.

Jackson wedged himself against the doorframe and fired on the

Mechs to keep them away from the shuttle. "Hurry it up," he yelled. He drilled a Mech, then ducked into cover as two more returned fire, their rounds pinging off the shuttle's hull. When Jackson peered out again, the Mechs had vanished. "I've lost them," he yelled as Ten finally managed to fire up the engines.

"Manoeuvring and shit," said Ten, "hang on."

The shuttle lurched sideways, sending a Mech tumbling across the bay as it lost its footing on the hull. Bullets pinged and rattled against the hull, sending vibrations through the ship that were quickly drowned out as Ten blipped the engines and punched the thrusters to flip the shuttle around to face the doors.

"Argh!" yelled Jackson from the rear of the craft. "I'm still bloody here, you know!"

"Told you to hang on," said Ten through gritted teeth. "This ain't easy, you know. I'm doing it manually!"

"I can't get a line on the bastards," said Jackson as Ten twisted the ship again and nudged her forward. "We're moving around too much."

"What the fuck are you two playing at?" said Conway.

Ten looked around at the monitors until he found Conway's shuttle, *Stockton*, moving toward the open doors from the middle of the bay as a squadron of Mechs on discs fled into the open. "Just taking a last look around," he said as he nudged the shuttle's nose up.

"Well, we're off," said Conway, "and you need to get out of here too." *Stockton* slid through the open door and manoeuvred neatly to face *Vengeance*; then her main engines fired, and the shuttle disappeared from view.

"Shit! We really need to get out of here," said Jackson. "Look at the door!"

Ten flicked through the monitors until he had a view of the door. It was still locked shut, but through the hole, the Mechs had manhandled some sort of heavy railgun. As he watched, they set a tripod on the walkway, clamped its feet in place, and began installing the railgun.

"What the hell?" muttered Ten as the Mechs heaved a huge magazine onto the weapon and slotted it into place.

"Are we fucking going?" yelled Jackson as the railgun came to life and ran through a rapid auto-calibration routine, the barrel swinging first left to right, then up and down as it sought out threats to target. "Ten!" he yelled.

"I see it," said Ten, hands flying across the consoles as he laid in the flight plan. He glanced at the monitor one last time as the railgun spun to point directly at *Linthorpe*. Then he punched the control, and the main engines fired. The shuttle shot forward as the railgun spat fire.

Ten was slammed back into his chair. One monitor showed the rapidly approaching bay doors as *Linthorpe* blasted ahead; another showed the railgun twisting on its tripod to follow, firing continuously.

"Argh!" said Jackson from the rear of the ship. Then the engines cut out and the manoeuvring thrusters fired to point the shuttle towards *Vengeance*. "Are we cle–" Jackson managed before the engines fired again and he was smashed against the wall again.

"What?" yelled Ten, a joyful tone in his voice. They were clear, free from the Sphere and on their way back to *Vengeance*. "We're away," he said. "Kippers in the mess on *Vengeance* in thirty minutes, my friend."

"Oh, good," said Jackson weakly, "can't wait."

The view ahead showed a distant *Vengeance*, hanging in the dark against the stars. *Stockton*, a tiny point of light a couple of kilometres closer to the battleship, was close to the halfway point of her journey.

"Going home," said Ten quietly. He was tired, so tired. It would be good to get a decent meal, a change of clothes and a few hours of sleep.

Then a warning lamp flashed on one of the monitors. Ten leaned wearily forward and tapped it, as if that was going to make any difference, then flicked into the details of the report.

"Looks like they might have got a couple of solid hits in," he said, frowning at the monitor. "Life support's offline and, er, some of our sensors."

"Anything vital?" asked Jackson.

"More vital than life support?" said Ten. "Nothing we can't live without in the short term. Looks like we were lucky."

"Makes a nice change," said Jackson. "So we just sit back and wait?"

"Yup, but don't take the suit off, ok?"

"I live in this thing," snorted Jackson. "Not sure it'll come off if I try."

Then a channel opened from *Vengeance*, and the hairs on the back of Ten's neck stood up.

22

"So this is personal?" said Conway asked. "All of these deaths, all this destruction. It's because your ex-wife is hacked off with everyone and everything?"

The ready room on *Vengeance* was silent as the echoes of Conway's question died away.

"Phoenix had been pushed to extremes of endurance," said Stansfield. "She was side-lined by the Commonwealth and, quite frankly, I could have done more to support her. Our marriage was rocky, our work was difficult, and then the death of our son, Michael." He trailed off for a few seconds before pulling himself together.

"Michael's death was the final straw. There was already a group of disenfranchised engineers preparing to leave Earth on an Ark ship, and I think for her, it was an escape. She was desperate to leave it all behind. The last words she said to me were '*You killed our son and betrayed me. I can never forgive you, and there will be a day of reckoning for this.*'"

There was more silence.

"We have to make contact," said Conway. "Talk her out of this, make her see sense."

"We're trying," said Vernon, "but they aren't responding. They don't seem interested in making polite conversation."

"She'll come for me," Stansfield interrupted. "Why else do you think that *Vengeance* hasn't been destroyed? They could have destroyed the ship at any time, but instead they allowed our ship to survive. There's a reason for that."

"They're still trying pretty fucking hard to kill us over here," snapped Conway. "Sir," she added as an afterthought.

"But what then?" asked Davies. "After they kill you, sir, what's her next step?"

Stansfield glanced at Vernon, then sighed. "She always said she'd return to Earth. The fact she's still alive after all these years indicates that she's either been in stasis – waiting – or she's found some way to prolong her life. I'm guessing the Mechs are the clue. But who knows what she wants, apart from revenge for the death of our son?"

"We have to go out there," said Davies. "If they won't talk to us, we have to knock on the front door and force our way in. She can't have held that anger for over a century; there must be another reason they're being so aggressive. They have skin in the game. They've lost too many Mechs to waste more."

"Davies is right," urged Conway. "Now Phoenix is here, we board her ship and open a dialogue."

Stansfield nodded thoughtfully, then looked at Vernon.

"I agree with Conway and Davies," said the commander. "I knew Phoenix too, and I can't believe all this hatred sprang from Michael's death. There has to be another reason."

"Fine," said Stansfield, "we board and open a dialogue, but no more half measures. I want Charlie Team to deploy as one unit, properly equipped and with whatever backup is needed to make this work."

"We're a bit spread out at the moment, sir," Conway pointed out.

But the admiral was having none of it. "Get back to *Vengeance*, Conway. That's an order. We'll prep an assault craft and plan a distraction to cover your departure. We only get one shot at this, so you're taking the full team, and I want you fully prepared."

"Understood," said Conway, although there was still doubt in her voice. "We're boarding now, with you in forty minutes. Out." Conway and Davies disappeared from the channel, and Stansfield looked around the room.

"Lieutenant Fernandez," he said, now firmly back in control, "I want an update on my engines and weapon systems in twenty minutes."

"Understood, sir," said Fernandez, standing up. "I'll check with Warburton, then update you." He hurried from the room and disappeared across the bridge.

"Captain Pierce, how long till *Defender* joins you?"

"Fifteen minutes, sir," said Pierce.

"Very good. Hold your side of the portal at all costs, and let nothing through that isn't one of our own, understood?"

"Stand our ground, destroy all aggressors," Pierce summarised. "Understood. *Conqueror* out." Pierce dropped out of the channel.

There was a brief moment of silence; then the admiral turned to Lieutenant Woodhall. "I want you, Lieutenant, to continue your work with the crew of *Orion*. Get them settled in and ensure they are assigned quarters and duties. That is all."

Woodhall frowned and opened his mouth, but Captain Ryan spoke over him. "That sounded like an order, Lieutenant," said Ryan coldly, "and you would be well-advised to follow it." He stared blandly at Woodhall, but his eyes danced with anger.

"Very good, sir," said the lieutenant, his tone leaving no doubt that he thought his orders anything but good. He left quickly, leaving only Yau, Stansfield, Ryan and Vernon at the table. The admiral waited until the door slid closed before speaking again.

"Davies' plan is brave but flawed," he said, speaking quietly and quickly, "and I have no intention of sacrificing them to cover up my mistakes. Captain, you're ready to proceed?"

Ryan looked up and nodded. "*Orion's* self-destruct sequences have multiple redundant backups and are considerably over-engineered. They'll work, even with the ship in her current state."

"The enemy has teams on *Orion*," pointed out Vernon. "What happens if they interfere with the process?"

Ryan made a face. "That would be unfortunate," he said eventually, "but you need the command keys to alter the settings. Any attempt at interference once the time is running is interpreted as hostile action."

"So we just need to set the self-destruct mechanism and retire to a safe distance?" said Stansfield.

"Yes, which means getting at least thirty kilometres away," said Ryan, "and preferably a hundred. And I can set the mechanism with any of my senior officers once we get to the bridge. The shuttle is prepped, we're just waiting for the right time."

"I think that time might have arrived," said Vernon, nodding at the screen. The tactical overview showed Phoenix's ship at the centre of the huge armada, with a pair of battleships breaking away to head for the portal. "If we wait any longer, they'll overwhelm *Conqueror* and *Kingdom 10*."

"No, they'll be through the portal before a shuttle could return from *Orion*, sir," said Lieutenant Yau, gaze locked on his data slate as he ran the calculations. Then he frowned and looked up. "The journey to *Orion* will take at least thirty minutes, sir."

Ryan stood up and nodded. "Then there's no time to lose. I'll be on my way, sir," he said to Stansfield.

"No," said Stansfield sharply. "You heard Yau, there isn't time."

"I won't just sit here and lose, sir," said Ryan angrily. "We have to do something."

"And we will. The plan is solid," said Stansfield, "but you're not in the right place to execute it, Captain."

"I'm the commanding officer," snapped Ryan, "it has to be me who gives the command."

"No, Ryan," said Stansfield unhappily, "it just has to be someone that *Orion* recognises as her commander."

Ryan frowned and stared at the admiral, confused.

"Who's still out there, Lieutenant?" said Stansfield.

Yau frowned and consulted his data slate. "Conway and Davies are on their way back to *Vengeance* with Captain Figgis and the remains of his company. Marines X and Jackson are following some way behind in a separate shuttle. Haworth is out there with the remnants of his squadron, and, er, that's it."

"Marines X and Jackson are–" Stansfield began.

"You can't be serious!" snapped Ryan, smashing his fist down on the table. "A Penal Marine in command of a battleship? The very idea is–"

"Ludicrous?" said Stansfield. "I don't disagree, Captain, but it's the only way."

"They're the only ones who can get there in time, sir," said Lieutenant Yau, "and they're the best people to fight their way to the bridge, if that's needed."

Ryan glared at Yau for several long seconds, looking like he might explode with anger. Then he seemed to deflate as he realised the truth of the lieutenant's words. He nodded and sank back into his chair.

"Give Marine X the good news, Lieutenant," said Stansfield, picking up his data slate. "And impress upon him the urgency of the situation. Tell him we'll clear his outstanding sentence if he completes the mission."

"Aye, sir," said Yau, standing up. "And," he paused, suddenly uncomfortable, "I'm sorry for the loss of your son." He ducked out of the ready room before the admiral could reply, opening a channel to Marine X and Jackson as he went.

The admiral sat for a moment; then he looked expectantly at Ryan. "You have paperwork to do, I think?" he said eventually. "A pair of rapid promotions to force into *Orion*'s management systems? Lieutenant Yau will help with the technicalities."

Ryan took a deep breath and nodded. "Sir," he said. Then he was gone, following Yau back to the bridge.

"And what do you want me to do, sir?" said Vernon when the two of them were alone.

"Keep it together out there, Ed," said Stansfield. "Make this plan work so that we all have a home to go back to at some point."

Vernon nodded and stood up. He walked to the door, then turned back as it slid open. "And you, sir?" he asked quietly. "What will you do?"

Stansfield blew out a slow breath and picked up his data slate. "I'm going to make a call, Ed, and buy us some time."

23

"Marine X, this is Lieutenant Yau. We have a small job for you."
Ten glanced at Jackson, who was now sitting in the co-pilot seat on *Linthorpe*'s tiny flight deck. Jackson shrugged and said quietly, "How bad can it be?"

"Go ahead, Lieutenant," said Ten wearily. "I'm listening."

"The Mechs' main armada has arrived," said Yau. "I'll spare you the details, but we can't let them reach the portal. It has to be destroyed."

"Let me guess," said Ten. "You want me to do something dangerous that'll save the day and destroy the portal?"

"We want you to board *Orion* and trigger the self-destruct mechanism," said Yau, ignoring Ten's question.

"I knew we shouldn't have taken this call," muttered Jackson, shaking his head.

"You want me us to board a terminally-damaged battleship, find the self-destruct mechanism in the face of a hostile enemy, and then what? Escape back to *Vengeance*?" said Ten.

"That's about the size of it," said Yau apologetically.

"I have to say I'm not desperately keen on this plan, sir," said Ten. "Is there no other way to–"

"There's no time for anything else, Marine X," said Yau desperately. "The first Mech battleships will cross the portal in fifty-four minutes, the next six minutes after that. You're about twelve minutes from *Orion*, eight minutes to get to the bridge, eight to get back to the shuttle, and then twenty to reach *Vengeance* with six minutes to spare. I'm sending you a new flight plan." A chime sounded in Ten's HUD as a new file arrived.

"That's a pretty tight plan," said Ten. "What happens if something goes wrong?"

"I'm sorry," said Yau, "we're out of time. If the Mechs make it through the portal in numbers, they'll wreak havoc."

"Yeah, I get it," said Ten.

"The admiral has promised to have your outstanding sentence cancelled and restore you to full duty if you complete the mission."

"He'd better fucking not," snapped Ten indignantly. "Have you any idea how hard I've worked to get to my current position?" But even as he spoke, his hands were flicking at the shuttle's controls, laying in the new flight plan.

"I'm sending everything we know about *Orion*'s internals to your HUDs," said Yau. "She's a wreck, the power's off, and it's full of Mechs."

"Lovely," muttered Ten.

"Anything else you need?"

"Just tell Stansfield he'll owe me for this," said Ten, "and don't let him forget Jackson when he's handing out the gongs, okay?"

Jackson snorted and shook his head again.

"I'll do that," promised Yau. "It'll be promotions all round if we get through this."

"Yeah, yeah, heard it all before," muttered Ten as he ran an eye over the flight plan. "Be seeing you, sir."

Then he punched the trigger and *Linthorpe*'s manoeuvring thrusters fired, swinging her around to begin the short journey to *Orion*.

∾

O n *Vengeance*, Stansfield sat alone in his ready room, staring at the tactical overview on the main display. The armada was manoeuvring into columns in front of the portal, which had now stabilised at four times its original size, large enough for even the biggest of the enemy ships to pass through.

And they were operating without the slightest fear of either *Orion* or *Vengeance*. It was as if the two ships were completely irrelevant.

Stansfield snorted. Of course they were irrelevant. He'd have dismissed them, if their positions had been reversed.

Conqueror seemed to be having more impact. The Mechs had stopped sending small squadrons through the portal, but whether because they'd learned all they needed or because the losses were too great, Stansfield couldn't tell. Now they were lining up their battleships, dozens of them, and there was little doubt that *Conqueror* would be overwhelmed once the attack began in earnest.

A channel request arrived from Lieutenant Fernandez, and Stansfield accepted it quickly. Even bad news was worth hearing, if it delayed the inevitable confrontation.

"Sir, an update on the engines and weapons," said Fernandez. "It's not good news. We'll need at least sixty hours to get the engines online. We'll have a second railgun battery in maybe ten hours, but until the factory units are brought online, our ammunition will be very limited."

"Thrusters, Lieutenant?"

"Er, no, sir. Sorry. There's just too much damage," said Fernandez. "But the hyperspace drive is working."

"Thank you, Lieutenant," said Stansfield. "Keep working on it." He closed the channel and sat back to think.

"No escape," he muttered eventually, staring at an image of the portal on one of the room's displays. The tactical overlay showed only thirty-two minutes till the first pair of Mech battleships passed through the portal.

Stansfield sighed and picked up his data slate. One of the engineers had configured it to allow him to initiate hailing calls to the

Mechs, and now was the time. He set it on the desk so that he was in the camera's field of view, then checked there was nothing sensitive on the walls behind his chair. Finally, when he could delay no longer, he straightened his grubby uniform, ran a hand through his hair, rubbed his eyes, and pressed the initiate call button.

The response was almost immediate. No sooner had he settled back in his chair than the channel opened into a confused view of dark metal and pipework.

Stansfield blinked, unsure what he was looking at, and the view suddenly shifted to show a single Mech sitting in a huge command chair at the centre of a nightmare of cables and steel. He squinted into the slate, trying to make out a face amongst the shadows, to see any hint of something recognisably human.

For a long minute the two commanders stared at each other across the void, as still as statues and hardly breathing. Then the Mech shifted, and the light fell on its face.

Stansfield gasped. "Phoenix," he breathed.

It was her: there could be no doubt. The years had left her recognisable, but her hair had gone, and part of her skull glinted in the dim light. A thick bundle of cables disappeared into a steel plate in her skull, and when she leaned forward, the cables shifted like snakes in a pit.

She hissed, leaning forward as a snarl contorted her face. Her lips worked slowly, as if their owner was unfamiliar with their purpose or rediscovering them after long years of disuse. She tilted her head, and Stansfield blinked in surprise at seeing the once-familiar mannerism in something so grotesquely alien.

"I am the Primary," she said, and Stansfield's heart lurched at the pain and hatred in her voice, "and the time for vengeance has arrived!"

"Not so sure this is a good idea," said Jackson as *Orion* grew quickly on the monitors. The battleship was dark, lit only by the light from the nearest star and from the portal. "Don't see an easy way out of this."

"Are those Mechs?" said Ten, zooming in to get a better look. *Linthorpe's* cameras struggled with the distance, but the Mechs were clearly visible as they cut away pieces of *Orion's* hull. *Target Six* still floated above *Orion*, both ships looking like they'd seen better years and neither able to do more than bask in the starlight.

"Bloody scavengers," muttered Jackson.

"I'll take us around the far side," said Ten, hands on the console. "Keep us away from *Target Six* and the Mechs."

"Time's tight," said Jackson. He'd loaded a countdown timer into their HUDs alongside Yau's schedule. "We're eating into our contingency."

"Can't be helped," said Ten firmly. "We'll never get there if we have to fight our way through the entire Mech army. Twice, if we're going to escape."

"Probably find poor old *Linthorpe's* been disassembled for spares by the time we get back," said Jackson.

"Is there anything useful back there?" said Ten, waving his hand at the shuttle's hold. "I'm running short on, well, pretty much everything."

Jackson pushed himself out of his seat and floated back down the shuttle to take a look. "Oxygen, water, food, meds. Plenty of ammunition and grenades," he said, pulling open a crate and reloading his weapons. He stuffed more supplies into his webbing and his pack, then took armfuls of kit to Ten in the cockpit. *Orion* had grown noticeably larger in the brief time he'd been away.

"Any rocket-propelled grenades?" asked Ten as he checked his weapon and refilled his depleted webbing with magazines and grenades. "I reckon we could use the firepower."

"Can't see any. Looks like Figgis' team was travelling light."

"Yeah, figures," said Ten as he plugged his suit into the shuttle's waste management systems. The automated services cycled the suit's tanks and topped up on power, O2 and water. On the monitors, *Orion*'s hull loomed huge and grey as the shuttle slowed and twisted, heading towards the main bay.

"We'll dock at the edge," said Ten as *Linthorpe*'s main engines fired again to slow her to manoeuvring speed. "Then it's a dash through the abandoned halls to the bridge, set the self-destruct mechanism, then back to the shuttle."

"Right," said Jackson doubtfully. "What could possibly go wrong?"

"Yeah," agreed Ten. "Better pack some more ammunition."

Jackson appeared a moment later with another handful of magazines and stuffed them into Ten's pack. He peered at the monitor as Ten concentrated on guiding *Linthorpe* in through *Orion*'s open bay doors.

"Shit, more Mechs," he said, pointing at what looked like a welcoming committee in the bay. "They've seen us," he said as the Mechs opened fire with small arms.

"Whoa," said Ten, "too many." He spun the shuttle, getting the hang of her manual controls, and nudged her away from the open door. "Need another way in. Where's the bridge?"

Jackson flicked through the schematics Yau had shared until they popped onto *Linthorpe*'s displays, laid across *Orion*'s hull. "That's the bridge," he said, flagging a room towards the top of the battleship. "This is the nearest bay, though. All the others are too far away or too damaged for us to access."

"Then we go in through the hull," said Ten, blipping the thrusters to move *Linthorpe* closer to Orion. The battleship filled the display as Ten twisted the shuttle around and followed the curve of the hull. "There," he said, pointing at a spot that was mercifully free of Mechs, "we'll go in there."

"More bang-bang worms?" said Jackson.

"I wish you wouldn't call them that," muttered Ten. "It sounds ridiculous." *Linthorpe* twisted gently above the hull as he brought her to the landing point. The ship seemed to shudder as she touched the surface. Then her magnetic skids engaged, locking her to *Orion's* hull.

"Right on schedule," said Ten smugly as he slipped out of the pilot's chair.

"Hardly," said Jackson as he gathered thick lengths of plastic explosive. "Grab the detonators," he said, nodding at a box that floated near the ceiling.

Ten stuffed the detonators into his pack and slung his rifle as they made their way to the shuttle door. It slid smoothly open, and they looked out across the grey expanse of the hull as it curved gently away from them. Above, the stars glittered and beyond, only a few kilometres away, hung the portal.

"That's a view that never gets old," muttered Ten as the universe stared down at him. "Puts everything into perspective, doesn't it?"

"Sure," said Jackson, "it's smashing. Now, where exactly do you want to do this?"

Ten shook himself and turned his attention to the hull. "There," he said, pointing at a blank spot ten metres from *Linthorpe's* door. "If we cut a hole through there, we should be just outside the bridge. Simple."

Jackson grunted as he stepped onto the hull, boots clamping onto the surface to hold him in place. He took a few awkward steps forward, then glanced over his shoulder. "Ten! You coming?"

"Yeah, right, sorry," said Ten, shaking his head. He hurried to catch up, and the two Marines made their way across the hull, nothing above them but void. "Can we do a three-metre-wide square?"

Jackson looked over their supplies. "Maybe one and a half," he said as he knelt on the hull and began laying out the explosives. He pressed one of the lengths of explosive onto the hull, and it shattered under his fingers. "Shit," he said, as the material floated free. He tried again, and this time a small cloud of powder formed as the frozen explosive cracked and split. "This isn't going to work, it's too cold."

"Shit, should have thought of that," said Ten. "Any ideas?"

"Nothing," said Jackson.

"You got any more of that canned stuff we used earlier?" said Ten.

"No, that was the last of it, and there wasn't any in the shuttle," said Jackson.

They were silent for a moment; then Ten opened a channel to *Vengeance*. "Lieutenant Yau? We have a problem," he said. He gave a quick summary of the situation. "We need a way into the ship."

"And what do you expect me to do about it?" snapped Yau.

"Find me a way into the ship," said Ten slowly, "or this whole idea's shot." The channel went quiet. "Hello? Hello? Anyone there?"

"I'm working on it, Marine," said Yau. "Shut up and let me think." The channel went dead again.

"I guess we wait," said Ten, looking up from the hull and peering off into the distance. Something moved, and he frowned as his HUD magnified the image. "Oh, come on," he said, exasperated. Then he unslung his rifle and peered through the scope.

From the edge of the ship, a pair of Mechs approached, and behind them were two more.

"Company," said Ten feeling unbelievably ancient and tired as he aimed.

Jackson looked up and swore. "They just don't give up," he said, aiming his rifle. "Ready?"

"Short, controlled bursts," muttered Ten, squeezing the trigger. The first two Mechs exploded in a spray of bodily fluids and stopped moving, their suits still clamped to *Orion*'s hull. The next pair shifted sideways. One ducked into cover behind some sort of sensor array. The other stopped, one leg raised, as holes appeared in its chest.

"Anytime now, sir," said Ten as he took a step sideways, trying to bring the fourth Mech into view. Then two more Mechs appeared, firing as they came, and things got a little more difficult.

24

"It's good to see you again," said Stansfield. His voice was hoarse and his heart was beating so hard he was almost sure she could hear it. He'd never imagined their reunion might be like this; he'd never really thought they'd see each other again.

Certainly not like this. She was attached by a series of tubes and cables to a mass of equipment around her. She was the most human of the Mechs they'd seen, but she was completely dependent upon the bank of tech and medical racks to which she was attached.

"I thought you were dead," he said quietly.

"You *hoped* I was dead," snarled Phoenix, her part-synthesised voice crackling with anger, "but here I am."

"No, not 'hoped', never that," said Stansfield. "Feared. All those years you were missing; then you showed up, stole a ship and disappeared again. A decade of fear and dread, never knowing where you were or what you–"

"Lies!" she said. "All lies. You never cared. You sent our son to his death and all you cared about was your precious experiment."

"No," said Stansfield angrily, "that's not–"

"Enough," she shouted. "You cared about your career, nothing else. Not me, not Michael, not the people who served under you. It was only ever your career that mattered."

"No," hissed Stansfield, "no!" But he knew she was right. "I'm sorry. Let's talk, please. We can resolve this. It doesn't have to end like this."

"The time for talk is long gone," the woman shouted.

"I want to apologise – I *need* to apologise – for the death of our son," said Stansfield. "For pushing you away, for arguing against you and pressing on with the experiments in spite of your warnings. You were right, and my actions killed our only child. I'm sorry, Phoenix–"

"You will not call me by that name!" she screamed, leaning out of her chair so that the tubes and cables behind her bounced and stretched. "I am the Primary!"

"You don't have to do this," he said earnestly. "I'm here. I'll surrender. Punish me, if I'm the cause of your anger, but spare my crew. Neither of us needs to lose any more of our people."

"Be quiet!" she seethed at him. "You always thought it was about you, but now you'll watch your planet burn. Everything you had, everything you dreamed of, everything you value, we will take! You have grown fat and weak, while we have grown strong and numerous." She sat back in her seat, breathing heavily. "We will take your planet."

"But why?" said Stansfield. "You must see how crazy this is, Phoenix."

"I am the Primary!" she screamed at him.

Stansfield held up his arms, leaning back from the slate as she raved. "I can't let you do this," he said. "You will not be allowed to pass through the portal."

She paused, staring at him; then she tossed back her head and laughed. Stansfield ached at the memories her laughter brought back, but this wasn't the way he remembered it. She had been warm and loving; now she was cold, heartless, mechanical.

"The ships you've sent through the portal have been destroyed," he said, ignoring her laughter. "Our forces are in position; you cannot hope to break out once you pass through the portal," he said with a confidence he didn't feel.

"You idiot," she said, all mirth stripped away. "You think I care about a few flights of scout ships? A few battle cruisers? The Spheres?"

Stansfield frowned and opened his mouth, but she wasn't done.

"You think this is it?" she asked, waving her hands to indicate her fleet. "You think this is everything?"

Stansfield closed his mouth as a sudden chill engulfed him. She'd never been one for bluffing – what you saw was what you got – but she always planned in layers. His gaze darted to the other displays, searching for something he'd missed.

"You are a fool," she said, leaning forward again, claw-like fingers locked on the arms of her chair. "You see what is before you and miss everything else. This isn't my full strength. This isn't a tenth of one per cent of what I'll bring to bear on your puny Commonwealth."

"No," breathed Stansfield with a slow shake of his head. "That's not possible."

"Ha! You dare tell me what's possible? You, constrained by your rules and guidelines and laws? You, who abandoned me when you couldn't see the truth? I will show you what a century of uninhibited progress looks like," she snarled. "I'll show you what can be achieved with drive and determination!"

"And the best minds the Commonwealth had to offer!" snapped Stansfield. "Oh, yes, Phoenix. Don't think it went unnoticed that you took our best and brightest when you started this mad scheme. Nothing you've achieved would have been possible without them!"

They glared at each other for several seconds; then the Primary sat back, forced her fingers to release their grip, and drew herself into a regal pose. "Your words no longer matter," she said eventually. "And neither do you. Your ship is broken, your allies lost or dead, and soon we will begin the conquest of the Commonwealth."

The connection broke, and the comms screen went blank. For a moment, Stansfield was still; then he took a deep breath and shuddered. He was sweating, and as he wiped his forehead he realised just how tired he was.

~

"There's an airlock," said Yau, after what seemed like hours but was, in fact, only a few minutes. "Twenty metres to starboard, ten to aft."

"Roger," said Ten as the route appeared in his HUD. Superimposed on the hull, it ran right past the Mechs. Ten sagged down against the hull and looked at Jackson. "You seeing this?"

"Pretty much as I'd expected," said Jackson.

"Hurry it up, Marines," said Yau. "We're running out of time."

"Noted," said Ten, muting the channel. "What does he want, magic?"

"So, how do you want to do it?" said Jackson. They were both pinned down, each flat against the hull to keep out of sight of the Mechs. A stalemate, but the Mechs had all the time they needed.

"Grenades," said Ten, pulling a pair from his pack and setting them on the hull. "Link them to your HUD, toss them gently across the surface of the hull, detonate them at the appropriate point, then charge in firing."

"You want to charge?" said Jackson as he fiddled with his grenades. "Can't see that working."

"Well, just waddle as fast as you can and try not to get killed," snapped Ten. "Ready?"

"Sure," said Jackson, "why not?" He tossed his grenades, watching them float in a flat trajectory across the surface of the hull. Ten waited a few seconds, then sent his after them.

"And bang," said Jackson, detonating his grenades. Two Mechs were shredded by shrapnel, their corpses floating free from the hull.

"And waddle!" said Ten as his own grenades exploded. He released the clamps holding him on the hull without waiting to see what damage his grenades had done, and heaved. He skimmed across the surface of *Orion* like a demented superhero, flying a few inches from the hull as Jackson strode angrily forward, rifle raised.

As he neared the Mechs' position, Ten reached out a hand and caught a knob on the surface of the ship. Spinning, he landed on his feet, clamped himself firmly in position, and opened fire on the stunned Mechs who still loitered around the open airlock.

Moments later, Jackson arrived, but by then the Mechs were all dead and either floating away into the void or standing like statues, their suits forever locked in place.

"'Waddle', eh?" said Jackson as he moved cautiously to peer into the airlock. It was empty, and the inner door was open so that it was possible to see directly into the ship's corridor.

"Seemed appropriate," said Ten as he peered into the airlock. "Shall we?"

"Oh, no, please, after you," said Jackson politely.

"Right," said Ten. He spun neatly around, then pulled himself head-first into the airlock, rifle at hand. Jackson waited on the hull until Ten had cleared the inner door, then followed as quickly as he could.

"Jackson, Marine X," said a voice, "this is Captain Ryan. *Vengeance* has no motive power. We can't collect you, you have to reach us before *Orion* detonates."

"Understood, sir," said Jackson.

"Hold on," said Ten, frowning to himself, "how'll *Vengeance* make it through the portal without engines?"

There was a pause. "Just get here in time, Marines," said Ryan. Then the channel closed.

"This mission is going from bad to worse," muttered Ten.

"And we're six minutes behind schedule," said Jackson as he scanned the corridor, "so that's us nicely fucked, then."

"That way," said Ten, ignoring Jackson to push away from the airlock door and float quickly along the passage. The corridor was broad, and would have been brightly lit if *Orion* hadn't been one step from the breaker's station. With the power off, the passage was as dark and grim as anywhere Ten had ever seen.

"Five metres, two, there it is," said Ten as they reached the door to the bridge. "Dead," he snorted, "this ship's as reliable as *Dreadnought*. We'll have to crank it by hand," he said, flipping open the panel and reaching for the lever. He cranked it back and forth, slowly levering the doors open. When there was a metre-wide gap between the two doors, Jackson peered in and shone his helmet lamps around the bridge.

"Clear," he said with no small degree of surprise. "Where've they all gone?"

"Don't know," said Ten as he floated into the bridge, "don't care. Captain Ryan," he said, opening a channel back to *Vengeance*, "we're on the bridge. Where's the self-destruct trigger?"

"There are two. The first is in a panel in front of the command chair," said Ryan. "The second is above the science station. Lieutenant Yau is giving you command rank on *Orion*. Marine X will be Acting Captain; Jackson will be the Acting Chief Science Officer."

"Long time since I've done any officering," said Ten absent-mindedly. He pushed across the bridge as Jackson watched the corridor.

"Don't let it go to your head," said Yau drily. "It's strictly temporary."

Ten grunted and caught hold of the command chair. On the floor, beneath his boots if he'd sat in the chair, was a panel, just as Ryan had said. "It's locked," said Ten as he pulled on the panel's handle. "You want me to shoot it open, or something?"

"No!" snapped Ryan. "It just needs the command code." A packet of information arrived in Ten's HUD. "Link to the self-destruct system's network and give it that code. That'll unlock both panels, then you each need to give command authorisation within a single thirty-second window."

"Thirty seconds from one command authorisation till the other?" said Ten as he linked his HUD to the self-destruct system's private network and prepped the panel key.

"Thirty seconds from opening the panels," snapped Ryan. "And there's a four-hour cooldown period, so don't fuck it up!"

Ten paused and glanced up at Jackson. "Let me just close the door," he said, cranking the lever, "and we should've been back on the shuttle by now." The doors slid slowly together, and Jackson pushed his way across the bridge to the science station.

"Ready?" said Ten as a second key file arrived in his HUD.

"Got my key," said Jackson, "and I'm at the science station. Good to go."

"Here goes nothing," said Ten. He fed in the first key and the panels popped open. Beneath the panel, a timer began to count down from thirty seconds, and a new piece of UI appeared in his HUD, ready to receive the two command keys.

"And now for the second key," said Ten.

"No, wait," said Yau. "I haven't finished the command updates."

"Twenty-four seconds," said Ten.

"Shit," said Yau, and Ten could practically hear the panicked lieutenant working in *Orion*'s much-abused back-end systems.

"Fifteen seconds," Ten said conversationally. "Anything we can do to help?"

Jackson shook his head and raised his rifle as the doors began to inch open. "We have company," he said, firing a couple of rounds through the gap between the doors.

"Five seconds," said Ten. "Cutting it a bit close, sir."

"Now," shouted Yau, "do it now!"

Ten pushed the second key into the commander's slot and punched the physical button beside the counter. In his HUD, the UI went green; then Jackson's key appeared in the other slot and it flashed red before vanishing.

"Is that it?" said Ten. "Or do we have to sit in the dark for four hours?" He looked down at the counter beside the trigger button, but it was blank and dead.

"I did my bit," said Jackson, waving his hand at the Science Officer's panel and the button it had hidden. "What do we do now?"

Then the door slid a little further open, and a gun barrel appeared. There was a pause; then the muzzle flashed as the Mechs began to fire indiscriminately into the room. For a moment, Ten and Jackson were distracted by the sudden firefight.

"Have they gone?" said Jackson when the Mechs stopped firing.

Then a new icon popped into Ten's HUD. A timer on a line drawing of *Orion*.

"Thirty minutes till she blows," said Ten. He stared at the time for a moment, blinking. "That's long enough for us to get back to *Vengeance*, but the Mechs will make it through the portal. Too long."

"You need to get off that ship, Marines," said Lieutenant Yau, "and back to *Vengeance*. We need to get clear of the blast zone, and we can't pick you up."

"But we're late," snapped Ten. "Thirty minutes is far too long."

"It's the default setting," said Ryan, "and you need that long to get to *Vengeance*."

"But the Mechs will make it through the portal, sir," protested Ten.

"Nothing can stop that now, Marine," said Ryan, his voice laden with defeat and loss. "All we can do is minimise the damage."

"How long till the first ship crosses?" demanded Ten.

"I don't see how that's relevant," snapped Ryan.

"How fucking long?" yelled Ten. "Sir."

"Sixteen minutes, Marine," said Ryan, "and you'll be on a charge as soon as you reach *Vengeance*. Ryan out."

"Fuck you, sir," said Ten to the dead channel. He fired at the gap in the doors again, just for the hell of it. "Adjusting the timer," he said to Jackson, fiddling with the self-destruct system's UI in his HUD. The timer blinked and started counting down from fifteen minutes.

"Wait, what?" said Jackson, appalled. "That's not enough time to reach *Vengeance*. What have you done?"

But Ten was already heading for the doors, a pair of grenades in his hand. "We're not going to *Vengeance*," he said as he tossed the grenades into the corridor and readied himself beside the door lever.

Jackson stared, dumbfounded. "Then...where?"

25

The bridge of *Vengeance* was silent as they watched *Orion* being stripped by the Mechs and carried, piece by piece, to the waiting *Target Six*. On another screen, the Mech armada manoeuvred towards the portal. Battleships lined up in pairs, scores of them, nudging forward in neat order to play their part in the invasion of the Commonwealth. The feeling of defeat was palpable as Stansfield strode back onto the bridge and sat down in his command chair.

"How long on *Orion*'s timer?" said Stansfield.

"Fourteen minutes," said Lieutenant Yau weakly.

"Marine X adjusted the timer," said Ryan. "Cut their time in half."

Stansfield stared at the main display, where the shuttle *Linthorpe* could be seen clearly sitting on *Orion*'s hull. "How far are we from *Orion*?" he asked.

"Too far, sir," said Ryan. "Far too far."

"Is anyone else still out there?" said Stansfield.

"Haworth and the remains of his squadron," said Commander Vernon. "They're waiting to escort *Linthorpe* back to *Vengeance* once…" He trailed off. There was no way the shuttle could make it to *Vengeance* before *Orion*'s self-destruct mechanism destroyed the ship and incinerated everything within thirty kilometres.

"Get them back here," said Stansfield. "I want them in the bay in no more than ten minutes."

Vernon looked appalled, but the admiral stared him down. "Yes, sir," he said coldly.

"Midshipman Carter," said Stansfield. "Lay in a course. I want to be able to go as far from here as we can the moment I give the order."

"A course, sir? I don't understand."

"A course," snapped Stansfield, "through hyperspace, as far as we can go on our current power reserves. Is that clear?"

"Yes, sir," said Carter unhappily. "It's no more than a few light seconds."

"Then that'll have to do. Lay in the course, be ready to go on my command," said Stansfield as the atmosphere on the bridge turned cold and unfriendly.

On the main display, the counter ticked down to twelve minutes.

"And let's open a channel to Phoenix," said Stansfield. "I want to see if we can distract her a little from the matter at hand."

"Aye, sir," said Midshipman Campbell, "channel open."

The Primary responded to the channel request immediately, and a moment later her image flashed onto the main display. The bridge crew winced collectively as they saw Phoenix sitting in her command chair, a cybernetic counterpart to *Vengeance*'s more mundane version.

"Phoenix, it's time to talk," said Stansfield. "You can't win. Surely you must see that? What if our people could work together? What if we could negotiate a working truce?"

"I am the Primary," she thundered, "and there will be no truce, no collaboration, no peace."

"Yes, I know that's what you want," said Stansfield carefully, one eye on the timer, "but is that really the best course of action? Could we not come to some sort of arrangement?"

The Primary stared at Stansfield as if he'd gone mad. Then realisation flashed across her face and she looked away, staring around her own bridge before her attention returned to Stansfield. "What have you done?" she hissed.

"Me?" said Stansfield innocently. "You destroyed two of our

battleships in an unprovoked attack. I've only defended myself in the face of your hostility."

"Three," said the Primary distractedly.

"What?" said Stansfield.

The Primary turned to face him again, the glow of understanding on her face. "Three. You don't think your pathetic little vessel is going to escape, do you?"

Stansfield squirmed uncomfortably in his chair, and the Primary laughed. "Oh, you did. How quaint." She paused, and the humour drained from her face. "Time is almost up, Thomas."

"Well, you say that," said Stansfield, "but is it really true?"

The Primary looked away again, distracted by something that couldn't be seen from *Vengeance*. "You've done something on *Orion*," she said, her focus snapping back to Stansfield. "What have you done?" she snarled.

"You can't be allowed to win, Phoenix," said Stansfield sadly. "I have to stop you. I'm sorry."

She glared at him, then gave him a cold smile. "It doesn't matter," she said. "There's nothing to fear from that derelict hulk. But for you, night falls. Goodbye, Thomas."

The channel closed, and the tactical overview popped back onto the main screen.

"There's a pair of battleships manoeuvring into an attack position, sir," said Lieutenant Yau. "Ten minutes till *Orion* self-destructs."

"Designating them as *Target Seven* and *Target Eight*," said Pickering, her voice surprisingly calm.

"Ignore them," said Stansfield. "They're too far away to play any role in this. Focus on *Orion*."

The main display switched suddenly to show a section of *Orion*'s hull near the bridge.

"That's them, sir," said Pickering excitedly. "They're on the hull."

Two figures could be seen on the main display, clomping their way awkwardly across *Orion*'s hull, heading for the shuttle.

"They'll never make it," said Yau as *Linthorpe*'s airlock door closed and the shuttle's running lights came on. Across the hull, Mechs were appearing from *Orion*'s airlock, following the Marines. The flare of small arms fire was suddenly visible, and the bridge crew groaned.

Then *Linthorpe*'s thrusters fired and the shuttle bumped along the hull, leaving a long trail of sparks as she slid sideways. The Mechs stood their ground; then *Linthorpe* crunched over them, crushing them against *Orion*'s hull.

"I think Marine X is the pilot," said Yau. "Seven minutes."

"Does he even know how?" asked Ryan quietly.

But then the shuttle spun neatly, and began to travel slowly along the length of *Orion*'s hull.

"What is he doing?" said Stansfield with a frown, leaning forward in his seat. "Open a channel to that shuttle," snapped the admiral, "I want to know what the hell he's playing at."

"Channel open, sir," said Campbell.

"Marine X," said Stansfield, "would you care to explain where you're going?"

"Bit busy right now, sir," said Ten, "we're not alone out here."

Stansfield opened his mouth to shout at the Penal Marine, but Yau pointed at the main display. "Mechs, sir, on discs. *Linthorpe*'s being pursued."

"*Target Eight* has begun her attack run," said Pickering. "Estimate weapons range in seven minutes."

"You've got six minutes to get thirty kilometres clear," said Stansfield.

"So have you, sir," said Ten, "but we'll never reach *Vengeance*, even with working engines."

"You're going for the portal?" said Stansfield.

"Yes, sir," said Ten, "and it's going to be close."

"Then good luck," said Stansfield, "and we'll see you on the other side."

"Thank you, sir. Good luck to you too." The channel went dead, and the bridge crew watched *Linthorpe* skim past the end of *Orion*'s hull and twist around to face the portal. Then her engines fired and the little craft rocketed away.

"Will they make it?" said Stansfield, unable to tear his gaze away.

"Maybe," said Yau uncertainly, "but it's going to be very close."

Stansfield sat for a moment, then nodded.

"Sir, incoming channel request from the Primary," said Campbell.

Stansfield glanced at Vernon, who shrugged. "Is that course ready for me yet, Mr Carter?" Stansfield asked.

"Yes, sir," said Carter, "but–"

"That'll do nicely, Midshipman," said Stansfield. "Accept the request, Mr Campbell. Let's see what she has to say." He settled back in his chair and forced himself to relax as Phoenix appeared once more on the main display. "Phoenix, how lovely to hear from you," he said in a friendly tone. "Three times in a single day is almost too much for an old man to handle."

"I know what you've done on *Orion*," said the Primary smugly. "It isn't going to work."

Stansfield glanced at Ryan, who raised his hands to indicate he hadn't a clue what the Primary was talking about. On the display, the timer clicked past three minutes.

"I don't know what you–" Stansfield began.

"The self-destruct mechanism," said the Primary, and Stansfield felt a chill descend. "Ah, so you do know," she said, nodding as she watched the admiral's reaction. "You wanted to destroy the portal, to leave us stranded out here. But you've failed, just as you've failed at so many other things."

Stansfield held her gaze as Yau and Ryan worked at their terminals, inspecting and reviewing and trying to find out what the hell was going on.

"You, ah, you haven't interfered with the self-destruct mechanism on *Orion*, have you?" said Stansfield, allowing a tone of light concern to enter his voice.

"It is being disabled as we speak," said the Primary, "and then we will complete the destruction of your pathetic force before we sweep away the rest of the Commonwealth."

Stansfield shook his head sadly. "You're repeating your threats, Phoenix," he said, leaning forward with a concerned frown on his face. "That's a sure sign of a deranged mind."

The Primary boggled at him, then cut the channel. "She never was much good with constructive criticism," he muttered.

"The Mech battleships are accelerating," said Yau, glancing at the timer. "It's going to be close."

There was a sudden commotion at the edge of the bridge, and Conway appeared with the rest of Charlie Team and Marine Gray, all looking distinctly upset. Sub-Lieutenant Warburton trailed behind, looking no happier.

"What's going on?" Conway demanded. "That useless excuse for an officer won't let us onto the flight deck," she said, pointing at Warburton, "so we can't get to Phoenix."

"Ah, about that," said Stansfield. Admiral he might be, but he had the decency to look slightly embarrassed. "I lied. We're not negotiating, never planned to."

Conway worked her mouth soundlessly, unable to find the words.

"Three minutes till *Target Eight* is within range," said Pickering. "*Target Nine* thirty seconds behind."

"So where's Ten, then?" said Hunter. Then he saw the shuttle on the main screen, the only Navy ship still in the field, and his face fell as he made the leap. "Shit," he said, turning back to the admiral. "What's going on, sir?" he spat.

"Sir, signal from *Orion*," said Ryan, his face white. "Interference with the self-destruct mechanism."

"Hyperspace, Mr Carter, now!" said Stansfield.

"Aye, sir, activating now," said Carter, triggering the laid-in course.

The stars shifted and jerked as *Vengeance* dropped in and out of hyperspace.

"What have you done?" breathed Conway, eyes locked on the displays.

Stansfield ignored her. "Find the enemy," he snapped, "and turn everything off but the passive sensors. I want to run dark and silent."

"There they are," said Yau, updating the main display as the ship's systems fell silent around them. The screen flashed to show the portal, but so far away it was scarcely bigger than a pinprick. The armada, huge though it was, was made invisible by the distance.

"Zoom in, Lieutenant," snapped Stansfield, "we need to know what's going on."

"That's the best we can do, sir," said Yau. "We're just too far away, and the sensors are too degraded to get anything better."

"So how do–" Stansfield began.

Then there was a blinding flash in the centre of the display, and for several long seconds the screen was blank. When the image returned, *Orion* had gone, ripped apart in an orgy of fire and destruction, leaving nothing behind but an expanding shell of debris.

And the portal had gone.

EPILOGUE

Six hours had passed since the obliteration of *Orion*. Six hours of fear and desperate work as the crew of *Vengeance* had battled the ship's failing systems and fought to keep her alive.

Stansfield waited in his ready room as the officers filed in. They moved like zombies; dead-eyed and bone-weary, beaten down by the imminent threat of death. Each new arrival shuffled to the nearest free seat and slumped down, grateful to rest, if only for a few minutes. Lieutenant Fernandez arrived last, cast around for an unoccupied chair, then gave up and sat down on the floor.

"Our situation is dire," said Stansfield, "but it is not without hope. Lieutenant Yau?"

Yau nodded and looked around the room. "They haven't found us yet," he began, "so we can assume they're not looking."

Woodhall snorted. Of all the officers, he was the only one whose face wasn't grey from exhaustion and stress. "How do you work that out?" he demanded.

"Because we're only a few light-seconds from their position," snapped Yau, "and if they were actively searching they would surely have found us by now. They believe us to be beyond reach."

"Are they likely to find us?" asked Commander Vernon.

"No, sir," said Yau, "because we're far enough away that they can't easily see us, and with our emissions cut to almost nothing, we should blend in with the background. We're effectively invisible till we move."

"And how soon might we be able to do that, Lieutenant Fernandez?" asked Stansfield.

Fernandez looked up from his spot on the floor and flicked at his data slate. A model of the ship appeared on the room's main display. "This shows the damaged areas of the hull," said Fernandez as the model revolved. There was a lot of red. "And we have a list of the damaged systems; it's long. If we're careful, we should be able to manage a short hyperdrive jump in maybe six to twelve hours. Main engines will take a lot longer, even with the extra teams from *Orion*."

"And what about our other systems?" said Stansfield. "Weapons, life support, cloning?"

"The priorities are the hull and the hyperspace drive," said Fernandez. "Once they're flight-worthy, we'll be able to hide even more effectively and move if the need arises. Everything else is secondary."

"Days?" persisted Stansfield. "Or weeks?"

Fernandez was silent for a moment. "We're bootstrapping ourselves back to full function, sir. Swapping in new parts will take days, fabricating the parts we don't have will take weeks. I'll have a detailed plan for you in twenty-four hours."

"What about our other resources?" said Stansfield.

"We have some shuttles and a few other craft," said Haworth. "Nothing that'll get us home, though."

"Food, water and fuel are plentiful," said Yau. "If we continue to avoid detection, survival should be straightforward."

"We have working manufacturing units," said Fernandez, "so given time and raw materials we'll be able to fabricate pretty much anything."

"And we have plenty of cloning chemicals," said Ryan, "so once the bays are up and running we'll be able to re-deploy as many people as we have space to accommodate."

"What about Jackson and Marine X?" said Conway. "Is there any news?"

Vernon shook his head. "Nothing. We're too far away to see ships the size of their shuttle, and if they're still out there they're not broadcasting." He looked at Charlie Team and Captain Figgis. "We have to assume they're lost."

"Unless they made it through the portal," said Hunter.

"Speculation," said Vernon, "and there's no way to know till we're able to contact the Admiralty."

Stansfield nodded. "Which brings us to our next problem," he said. "What do we do next?"

Woodhall leaned forward as it meaning to speak but the admiral simply spoke over him to answer his own question.

"Our duty is clear," he said, answering his own question. "We must protect the Commonwealth, and that means preventing the Mechs from reaching Sol-controlled space."

"You propose to fight on?" asked Ryan.

"Indeed, Captain," said Stansfield with a slight nod.

"But what about getting home?" blurted Woodhall. "Do you expect to defeat the Mechs?"

"I expect every one of us to do their duty," said Stansfield. "We will fight, when necessary, but the path home will be long. You didn't ask for this. Neither did I, although the responsibility is mine." He paused for a moment. "The Primary must be stopped," he said eventually, "and that's our mission. Questions?"

The de-briefings were interminable. The same questions, over and over, as the story was broken into tiny pieces and put back together again. Ever second investigated, every detail checked, every action questioned.

"I thought the Mechs were bad," said Jackson when it was finally over and the two Marines were able to relax. He poured the rum and pushed a glass across the table.

"Nothing like a hostile inquiry to finish off a tough mission," said Ten, knocking back the rum and setting the glass back on the table, "but at least we made it back." He poured more rum and raised his glass. "Here's to those who didn't make it."

"Never forgotten," said Jackson, emptying his glass then pouring more rum. They sat in silence for a few minutes, sipping their drinks and enjoying the quiet of the mess.

"You know where you're going next?" said Jackson.

"Back to my previous posting," said Ten. "No rest, and all that. Can't really say any more. You?"

Jackson snorted. "This is going to amuse you," he said, not sounding at all amused. "Must have done something very wrong to get this posting."

"Now *that's* something I know all about," said Ten sympathetically. "Come on, spill the beans."

"The rest of my company's back on the other side of the portal," said Jackson. "With *Vengeance's* engines, even if she survived, it'll take them decades to get home. Nobody really knows where they are, so I'm being moved. Reassigned to that bloody museum, *Dreadnought*."

Ten coughed into his rum, but Jackson didn't seem to notice.

"Probably have me sitting behind a counter telling tourists where the exits are," Jackson grumbled. He looked up and frowned at the grin on Ten's face. "What's so funny?"

THANK YOU FOR READING

Thank you for reading Devastation Book 3 of By Strength and Guile, set in the Royal Marine Space Commandos universe.

We hope you enjoyed the book and that you're keen for us to write more books about Charlie Team, Vengeance and Admiral Stansfield.

Ten is going back to his other duties for now, but there are more of his adventures coming soon so make sure you're on our mailing list if you want to get hold of them.

It would help us immensely if you would leave a review on Amazon or Goodreads, or even tell a friend you think would enjoy the series, about the books.

Devastation is the second book in the By Strength & Guile series with our new co-author, Paul Teague. Paul is the author of many books, including the popular Secret Bunker & The Grid series.

We hope that you've enjoyed this first By Strength and Guile trilogy. We are already brainstorming ideas for more stories in the By Strength and Guile series.

If you'd like to read them, let us know about it. Paul is keen to get cracking on more books and your support is crucial. As long as we know there's demand for more books, we can get them out there for you.

We're also looking at collaborations with other authors so we can show The Deathless War on other fronts.

As always, thank you again for supporting our work and we wish you a happy New Year.

Jon Evans & James Evans

SUBSCRIBE AND GET A FREE BOOK

Want to know when the next book is coming and what it's called?

Would you like to hear about how we write the books?

Maybe you'd like the free book, Ten Tales: Journey to the West?

You can get all this and more at imaginarybrother.com/journeytothewest where you can sign up to the newsletter for our publishing company, Imaginary Brother.

When you join, we'll send you a free copy of Journey to the West, direct to your inbox*. You'll also get access to a free audiobook version, narrated by Steve West who has also narrated the main series.

There will be more short stories about Ten and his many and varied adventures, including more exclusive ones, just for our newsletter readers as a thank you for their support.

Happy reading,

Jon Evans & James Evans

We hope you'll stay on our mailing list but if you choose not to, you can follow us on Facebook or visit our website instead.

imaginarybrother.com

* We use Bookfunnel to send out our free books. It's painless but if you need help, they'll guide you through so you can get reading.

facebook.com/ImaginaryBrotherPublishing

twitter.com/imaginarybros

ABOUT THE AUTHORS PAUL TEAGUE

Paul Teague is the author of The Secret Bunker Trilogy, The Grid Trilogy and the standalone sci-fi novel, Phase 6.

He's a former broadcaster and journalist with the BBC but has also worked as a primary school teacher, a disc jockey, a shopkeeper, a waiter and a sales rep.

The Secret Bunker Trilogy was inspired by a family visit to a remarkable, real-life secret bunker at Troywood, Fife, known as 'Scotland's Secret Bunker'.

It paints a picture of a planet in crisis and is a fast-paced story with lots of twists and turns, all told through the voice of Dan Tracy who stumbles into an amazing and hazardous adventure.

The Grid Trilogy takes place in a future world where everything has gone to ruin.

Joe Parsons must fight for survival in the gamified Grid, from which no person has ever escaped with their life.

The standalone novel Phase 6 bridges the worlds of The Secret Bunker and The Grid, revealing what happens between Regeneration and Fall of Justice.

It depicts the world as we know it falling under a dark and sinister force - things will never be the same again.

Paul has been enjoying sci-fi since he was a child, cutting his teeth on Star Trek, Doctor Who, Space 1999, Blake's 7, Logan's Run and every other TV series that featured aliens, space ships and futuristic landscapes.

This collaboration with Jon and James Evans has allowed Paul to unleash his love of space ships and their crews.

He's a lover of Battlestar Galactica, Babylon 5, most iterations of Star Trek and Red Dwarf, and this series of books incorporate influences from all of those franchises and more.

Paul has also written thirteen psychological thrillers, including the best-selling, Don't Tell Meg trilogy and the brand new Morecambe Bay trilogy.

The Secret Bunker website can be found at **thesecretbunker.net**

The Grid website can be found at **thegridtrilogy.com**

You can find out more about Paul's sci-fi and thrillers at **paulteague.net**

Follow Paul on Facebook: **facebook.com/paulteagueauthor**

facebook.com/paulteagueauthor

ABOUT THE AUTHORS JON EVANS

Jon is a sci-fi author & fantasy author, whose first book, Thieftaker is awaiting its sequel. He lives and works in Cardiff. He has some other projects waiting in the wings, once the RMSC series takes shape.

You can follow Jon's Facebook page where you'll be able to find out more about the first five books of the Royal Marine Space Commandos series.

If you join the mailing list on the website, you'll get updates about how the new books are coming as well as information about new releases and the odd insight into the life of an author.

jonevansbooks.com

 f facebook.com/jonevansauthor

 a amazon.com/author/jonevansbooks

 g goodreads.com/jonevans

 BB bookbub.com/authors/jon-evans

 ⃝ instagram.com/jonevansauthor